To Fred

Kristen

Sex, Lies and Rock & Roll

KRISTIN DANIELS

ELLORA'S CAVE
ROMANTICA PUBLISHING

Lily's War

Everyone knows war is hell… Friends for years, lovers for only weeks, Lily is devastated when Eric tells her to not wait for him when he's recalled to active duty in Iraq. Now, after eighteen long months, he's finally come home.

But lives have changed, Lily has changed. All it took was one unexpected night in the arms of their best friend to make her see the light. Yes, she still loves Eric, but she's fallen in love with Zach, too. Waging her own private war, she sets out to prove to Eric that what she wants—what the three of them *need*—is a chance to build a life together.

Nobody ever said she had to fight fair to win.

Unscripted

Brynn Lang is already beyond nervous about getting naked in front of the camera for her first big Hollywood love scene, and the situation only worsens when her new co-star arrives on the movie set. No way can she rush into filming a passionate sex scene, not with the one man who broke her heart.

Fresh from a three-month stint in rehab, Ryan Manning is now clear, focused and ready to tackle this role of a lifetime. But there's more than just dollar signs and super-stardom enticing him. Brynn's here, looking sexier than ever. Ryan's determined to make amends for his drunk-assed mistakes and win her back, and he can't think of a better way to jump-start her desire than reminding her of the inferno that always raged between them whenever they touched.

But nothing's ever that easy. Brynn's furious and refuses to listen. This time, he's on his own. There's no script for him to follow. All he has is sincerity, honesty and love. He hopes to hell and back it'll be enough.

Chasing Eden

Graphic artist Eden Foster never expected a sexy game of hide-and-seek to turn into the hottest encounter of her life. The erotic dreams she's had lately starring to-die-for rock star Shane Tolan are almost enough to make her forget how badly she wants to design his next CD cover. Almost, but not quite. And now here he is in the flesh, ready to chase after her.

Shane likes to play dirty and he finally has Eden right where he wants her—outside on a balcony, tied to a chaise lounge and under his complete control. But he soon discovers it's not just Eden's body he wants, but the talented, business-savvy artist, too. Hell, he wants every luscious part of her.

When paparazzi's naked photos from that night show up on the internet, Eden is convinced her peers will believe she slept with the rock star just to design his CD cover. Shane knows nothing's further from the truth. And in order to prove it to her, he's going to have to show her his heart.

An Ellora's Cave Romantica Publication

www.ellorascave.com

Sex, Lies and Rock & Roll

ISBN 9781419961380

Edited by Raelene Gorlinsky.
Cover art by Syneca.

This book printed in the U.S.A. by Jasmine-Jade Enterprises, LLC.

Trade paperback publication August 2010

SEX, LIES AND ROCK & ROLL

LILY'S WAR

Chapter One

Eric Jameson knew he was going to break Lily Ward's heart tonight. The idea of actually doing it, however, ranked about as high as his willingness to get caught in the middle of an enemy sniper attack. But, honest to God, he couldn't see any other way around it.

Slumped in the front seat of his truck in the middle of her driveway, he stared through the dim evening twilight at the paper clutched in his hands. The paper that paved the way to Lily's heartbreak.

Recalled to active duty. *Goddamn it.*

He squeezed his eyes shut and thumped the back of his head against the rear window of the truck's cab. Every word on the paper was emblazoned behind his closed eyelids. No wonder though, since he'd stared at the orders so many times over the last few weeks. He knew each line by heart, especially the one that highlighted the date he was to report back to his unit, back to living hell.

March the fricking eighteenth. Tomorrow.

While everyone else he knew was out partying and getting drunk on green St. Patty's Day beer, here he sat in a beat-up truck with dread weighing heavy in his heart. Maybe he should've taken Zach up on his offer and headed over to the local bar for one last hurrah. But Lily had wanted this night together, wanted it to be just the two of them.

And Zach Howard—being Eric and Lily's best friend—more than understood their need for a little private one-on-one time tonight, so he hadn't pushed the issue, which was a good thing, Eric supposed. Lord knew he didn't need an audience for what he was about to do.

As an Individual Ready Reservist in the Marines, the possibility of being recalled always hung over his head. And now that the possibility had turned into stark reality, he felt to his bones the need to set things right. Some might call it morbid, but Eric was no fool. He'd spent more than half his last tour overseas. He knew the risks, the dangers. The all-too-real chance he may not come back alive.

All right, time to quit stalling. He sucked in a deep breath and forced his unease aside. Best thing would be to just go in there and do it. Rip the bandage off, so to speak. No sense dragging out how shitty this was going to be. How hard telling her not to wait for him would be.

He re-folded the orders, shoved them a little too forcefully into the glove box and then schlepped his ass from the truck up to her front door. With a quick knock, he twisted the knob and entered before she could answer, just like he always did.

The front room was dark, with only a few glowing candles to offer up any light. Soft music played in the background and the aroma from the lavender soap she used wafted delicately through the air.

As he stepped farther into her house, he couldn't help but think she'd somehow turned the tables on him. He smiled at the thought of her trying to set the perfect scene for him on his last night home, but then the smile faded for the same exact reason.

This could be his last night home.

He made his way down the short hallway and stopped at her bedroom door. It hung partially open, and when he set his palm against it to push it the rest of the way, he closed his eyes to prepare for what he imagined waited beyond it.

When he opened them again, he nearly faltered. He always considered himself to be a tough guy more or less, but the sight of Lily stretched out against a heap of pillows wearing a virginal white negligee had him ready to drop to his knees and beg for mercy, let alone for a reprieve from his unexpected orders.

"You're late," she said, then pursed a set of full lips to sip from a glass of champagne she held so gracefully in her hand.

He swallowed past his rising lust and took a guarded step into the room. God, how could he tell her not to wait for him when she looked like that? When every cell inside him screamed that he wanted her to do the exact opposite?

Her dark hair was tossed on top of her head in a mass of unruly curls, with several errant strands working loose and framing her face. And Christ, the negligee. The creamy satin—and the way the material barely covered those amazing breasts—was nearly enough to undo him.

She smiled then and his heart flipped at the same time his stomach flopped. She deserved so much more than what he had to offer her right now. She was so vibrant, so full of sensuality and possessed such a remarkable lust for life, he could never ask her to set aside all of that just to wait for him. Because he knew without a second of forethought that she would, and for her to do that—for her to put her needs and desires on hold—would only dim the vivacious spirit he so loved about her. Never mind what it would do to her if he didn't come home at all.

No, it'd be better for all of them if she forgot about the last few weeks, if she moved on and found someone else. If they went back to just being friends.

"Only by a few minutes," he finally managed.

She set the flute on the nightstand and crawled to the end of the bed. "A few minutes too long. I missed you."

Hell, if she missed him already… What in God's name would the next year or so be like for her? He didn't want to think about that, but when she rose to her knees and held out her hand for him to take, he couldn't think about anything else.

"Come here," she whispered, her sexy little grin back.

Lord, he wanted to reach out to her. The scents in the room, her in that goddamn sexy lingerie... His dick was practically bursting through his zipper already.

"Lil," he said, not moving a single muscle. Not daring to. "We need to talk."

She sat back on her heels, her outstretched hand drifting down and resting on her thigh as the smile fell from her lips. She stared at him, her breaths heavy, her swallows forced. But when her eyes welled, that's when he had to look away. He hated the thought of making her cry. He hated every single moment of this.

"I don't want to talk, Eric. Not now. Not unless it's you telling me how you're finally going to make love to me tonight. Or where on my body you're going to touch me."

And God, how he wanted to touch her, to make love to her. To memorize every inch of her and to ingrain every cry and moan into his psyche. He didn't want to forget a solitary thing about her.

He forced himself to look back at her. "It's important."

She shook her head, said, "Please," and held her hand out again. "I have a feeling I know what you're going to say. All I'm asking is for you to wait. Just take my hand and be with me tonight. Morning will come all too soon, Eric. We can talk then."

Yeah, they were going to have to.

He wanted to bash his head against the wall for wasting so much time with her before. She and Zach had been his best friends for so many years, yet he never said anything about the attraction he felt or the strong yearnings he held for her, not to either one of them. How could he? The last thing he needed was to ruin the camaraderie they'd all shared for so long.

But a few weeks back, he realized he couldn't stand not touching her any longer. So, despite the knowledge he could fuck up a treasured friendship, he took a chance. A chance that paid off in ways he never could've imagined.

And then he got recalled.

Irony was such a bitch. No way were the last few weeks with her even close to enough time.

He stepped up to the bed and she rose to her knees once again to wrap her arms around his neck. Her fingers toyed with the longer strands of hair at his nape. "They're going to make you buzz your hair off again, aren't they?"

She asked the question so nonchalantly, but her gaze never left his lips. He knew what she was doing. Avoiding. Avoiding discussing where his being recalled would leave them. He wanted to avoid it, too.

"Yeah, right after I report in."

He held her in his arms, his body lighting up from the fireworks she created inside him, from the smoothness of the satin negligee, from the heat of her equally smooth skin underneath. He roamed his hands over her back, needing to feel her everywhere, embedding it all in both his heart and his mind.

Even still, something inside him couldn't leave well enough alone. "Lil… I…"

She pressed a fingertip to his lips and then met his stare, unwavering. Determined. Damn, he loved her strength. Her passion.

"Shh. No more words, Eric."

He nodded, giving in a little too easily, but knowing in his gut it was because he wanted to touch her a million times more than he wanted to hurt her.

"For now," he reiterated, and then he kissed her.

Dear God…

He tasted the need on her lips, the rush of urgency as her tongue glided against his. Why in the hell had he waited so long to take her? This—her being in his arms, their bodies pressed so close together—was perfect. Perfection he could've been experiencing every morning, afternoon and night for the last month.

He rocked closer and pulled her in tighter. God, he couldn't get enough of her taste, of her fragrance. He scooped her into his arms and carried her around the end of the bed to the side. Setting her on her feet, he fisted the satin at her hips and pulled the material up and off. The negligee fell from his hand as he took in the heavenly sight she made.

He wanted to say something, anything. But instead he froze, too afraid of the three little words dangling a bit too precariously from the tip of his tongue.

Wait for me…

Rather than speaking those all-too-telling words, he smoothed his hands over her shoulders and feathered his fingers down her chest to her breasts. They were the perfect shape and size and fit within his palms as if she were made just for him.

Well, maybe she was.

The thought made his heart ache even more than his throbbing cock. He needed her, needed to be inside her. Wanted that connection to her for however long he could hold on to it.

He stroked his thumbs over her taut nipples and met her gaze. Her eyelids were heavy, her irises dark and glassy. A breathy gasp rushed from between her lips.

"On the bed." He recognized how the raw need for her had reduced him to single syllables, but he couldn't say any more. If he did, if he let loose the real thoughts rambling around inside his head…

No. He wouldn't.

She bit her lower lip as she sat on the edge and scooted back, doing as he said. He practically ripped the t-shirt off his body, didn't waste any time in shedding his jeans and boxers, either. He climbed on the bed, slid over her and covered her body with his. The heat, the electricity racing between them… *Sweet Jesus.*

He took her mouth again, insistent and on the verge of carnivorous. But she didn't seem to mind, if anything she seemed more in tune, more…

God, just more.

A need like he'd never known assailed him.

He loved it.

Hated it.

Cursed it.

Hands everywhere, they fought to touch each other, to cling to what they knew they were losing. Their bodies were tense, their muscles rigid and tight. A battle for sexual supremacy if he ever saw one. But it was a battle he'd irrefutably win.

A heady dominance surged through him. He grabbed her wrists, held tight and swept her arms above her head. He held her hands firmly within one of his, letting his control take over, his desperation for her show through.

"Eric," she groaned when he moved his lips to her chin, then lower past her neck to kiss along her collarbone.

The sultry way she said his name urged him on, gave him the justification to keep going. Good thing, too. He might just die right now if she told him to stop.

He grasped her hip in his free hand while he worked his lips lower. When he came to the rise of her breast, he kissed along the top and down the soft swell to the underside, circling around until he came to the center. With gentle pulls, he latched onto her nipple. When she arched into him, her heat, her wetness slicked along his abdomen. Christ, she was so ready for him. It took every bit of inner strength he possessed not to raise up and plunge right into her.

But there was something else he wanted even more. To taste her.

He released her wrists and cupped her breasts with both hands. He lavished attention on them, splitting his interest between both equally. Underneath him she writhed and moaned while tugging on his hair.

He chanced a look up to her face. Thick curls fanned the pillow, her eyes were closed, her lips slightly parted. He did his best to ignore the ache that one little look caused, and instead trailed kisses down her quivering stomach, nipped tiny bites along her hipbones. Sliding his hands down her thighs, he lifted her knees to spread her legs wider.

The width of his shoulders held her open for him, and he stopped for a moment to just stare. So pink, so pretty. She glistened just for him, *because* of him. This close to her core, the scent of her arousal made every ounce of his blood burn through his veins, made his cock pulse with a ferocious need for release. But he reined all that in—he had to, for her.

With a suddenly shaky finger, he traced along her labia before dipping inside her. She bucked under him, but he never let up. In, out… God, she felt so good. Tight. Wet.

His. At least until morning came.

When he added his tongue into the mix, she cried out and fisted the sheets at her sides. The flavor of her, of those luscious juices spilling over his taste buds… He dreamed she'd taste just like this. Sweet, like paradise dancing on his tongue.

He shouldn't have expected anything less.

He left no crevice of her pussy unexplored, locked every flavor he tasted and each sound she made into the steel vault in his mind, the one reserved only for memories of her. And when she came on a deep groan moments later, he locked every tremor away, too.

He waited for her to still a bit before he crawled back up her body, licking and kissing as he went. By the time he reached her neck, she was still panting and her eyes had drifted closed. But it was when she turned her head into the pillow that he caught sight of a single tear at the corner.

"Lil..."

She turned back to look at him with a sad smile. "I'm okay. Really," she said when he opened his mouth to speak again. "Don't stop. Please..." She reached over to her nightstand, and then pressed a condom in his palm. "I need you inside me."

When she cupped his cheeks and bit her bottom lip, he had to hold back a brokenhearted groan.

"Please, I want you. Now."

Now. Yes...*now*...

He wanted to. Shit, he *really* wanted to. But her tears... He was already hurting her and he hadn't even dropped the bomb yet.

"You're thinking too much, Eric. We knew... We both knew this wouldn't be easy tonight. But I want to be with you, no matter what comes later." She plucked the wrapper from his hand, ripped it open and reached between their bodies. The instant she touched him with the latex, he thrust into her hand to help roll the condom on.

When she drew her knees up, the action settled him right where he needed to be. With one hand he held onto her hip while he slid the other under her back and up to the nape of her neck to tangle in her hair.

He held her tight and kissed her hard, plunging his tongue into her mouth as he drove his cock in deep. A rush of heat enveloped him—a mimic of the electricity racing down his spine and around his balls. He staved off the need to come right then, stilled for just a second until he regained control.

God, how the fuck was he ever going to walk away from this?

When she shifted under him, he began to move, to drive and retreat over and over until he lost himself in her body, in the moment. He broke from her lips, sucked back a harsh breath and dove to her neck, still needing to taste her but needing air, too. He felt light-headed from their connection, from the power surging between them.

She cried out with each thrust inside her—his name, or God's, or any combination of the two. And with every shout she tightened on him further. Her hands on his shoulders, her latched ankles at the small of his back, and that sweet pussy around his cock.

He straightened his arms, hovering just above her. She stared back with her eyebrows drawn together and a sexy flush coloring her cheeks.

"We do this together. Look at me," he instructed when her eyelids drifted shut. "I can feel you. You're close, baby, aren't you?" When he shifted angles, she arched into him as a deep groan rose from her throat, a groan he unconsciously echoed. "Right there… God, right there. That's your sweet spot. *My* sweet spot."

"*Yes…*"

A deeper thrust, then another… His balls drew up tight, sweat broke out over his chest. He wanted to keep going, to hold off as long as he could, but when she reached that wicked edge of bliss, then a split-second later tightened around his cock with a pulsing rhythm so strong, he didn't have any choice but to follow. They came together, just like he'd wanted, with their groans in time with one another's, their bruising grips matched in the way they clutched the other's slick, sweaty skin.

He dropped to his elbows and buried his face against her neck as a quiet sob broke from her lips. But he couldn't—wouldn't—falter in his plans. Come morning light, he'd do what he had to do. As much as he hated the thought of it, he'd suck it up and tell her to move on.

With gentle strokes and tender kisses, he tried to calm her, all the while wishing for the first time in his life that the sun would fail to rise.

Chapter Two

"Will he come home?"

Zach closed Lily's refrigerator door and sighed. "You and I both know he'll do anything so he can. Bureaucracy being what it is, politics too… It takes time, Lil. Right now he's where he needs to be. TCB, babe. "

Taking care of business. Yeah, him and every other Marine out there. She hated where he was. Despised that he had to be there, so far away from home. So far away from her.

"He's been gone a little over a year now." She curled her legs under her on the couch and rested the wine glass on her thigh as Zach stood a few feet away in her tiny kitchen, pouring a beer into a tall pilsner. "He didn't think he'd be gone this long. And now I worry over how long it takes him to answer my emails anymore. Every response he sends back is so short. Clipped. Impersonal. It's like the second he stepped out of our lives and climbed into that damn plane, he became a new person. He's different now. Detached."

"He has to be." Zach took a slow sip of his too-full glass while making his way into the living room.

Oh, please. What macho crap.

"He loves me, I know it. How could he just leave like that?" She waved her hand in the air. "I realize it wasn't his choice to go. But why did he feel like he had to tell me to not wait? I would have. Still am, really."

She hadn't dated anyone since Eric left, didn't want to. He'd crushed her heart when he told her to move on, and she wasn't sure exactly how to begin repairing it. Dating random guys certainly wasn't the answer, the idea didn't even appeal to her. The only men she ever felt an attachment to were Eric and Zach. Her best friends. She simply didn't need anyone else.

Zach sat on the couch facing her and stroked a gentle hand up her calf. "Babe. You have to know why. He didn't *want* to do it, but I'm sure he felt it best at the time. He *does* love you. We both do. It was never a question of that."

She swiped at a pathetic tear as it slid down her cheek. "I replay that morning in my head all the time. You know, like maybe if I said this, or argued with him about that… I could've changed his mind."

"He caught you off guard."

She shrugged. "Somewhat. To be honest with you, I had a feeling. But I ignored it. I thought that after we… Well, after what we shared, he'd feel differently. Guess I was wrong."

Zach set their drinks on the table in front of them and slid her legs out from under her. He scooted up next to her and drew her into his arms.

"I just miss him, Zach. So much."

"Me too, Lil. Every damn day."

She snuggled into Zach's hold as he reclined a little more against the pillow propped up on the arm of the couch. His scent reminded her of Eric's—the smokiness, the masculine aroma of the outdoors. She loved it—both the reminder and being held by him. He always made her feel so secure.

Whereas Eric had always been her tough guy, the one she could count on to defend her with a quick show of force, Zach prided himself on being more of a wordsmith. Reasoning situations out by talking was his thing, even if he could easily rival Eric in the muscles department.

Zach was yin to Eric's yang. Opposing, but still so interconnected.

She burrowed deeper into Zach's arms and laid a hand over his taut abs, working it up and over his pecs until she covered his heart. The steady thumps against her palm soothed her even more. "He'll be home. Any day now, he'll come home."

He pressed his lips to her hair. "And until then, just keep him in your heart."

She closed her eyes, weary. Sad. "He never left it, Zach. He's always been there."

"As he should be," he said as she settled in further, relaxed and warm.

Wanted.

Zach woke to the warmth of Lily's body pressed against the length of his left side. The candles they lit had burned out, and the room was now aglow only by the flickering light of the television screen.

They both must've drifted off sometime during the movie, but he didn't mind. Not when he had such a rare opportunity to hold Lily in his arms.

He knew he should feel like a shit, like he was horning in on his best friend's girl, but something inside him knew that wasn't the case. Lily—in a lot of respects—had always been Zach's girl, too. He felt that deep in his heart. It's just that Eric had beaten him to the punch and claimed her for his own before Zach ever found the chance.

Before he'd ever found the *guts,* more like it.

Zach often wondered, if he'd been the one to confess first… What would've happened then?

And wasn't that the obstacle he faced now? Zach knew Eric's insistence that she find someone else would never change the way she felt, the way she still loved him. What if Zach wanted to throw his hat into the ring now, too? With the connection the three of them shared… Hell, even if they didn't see it, Zach did. And it was getting harder and harder to ignore.

Nevertheless, something in him felt as if he had to. He had to hold back, had to let them figure it out on their own.

He rubbed his lips over her forehead and looked down at her. Nestled the way she was in his arms, she looked so gorgeous and smelled so damn good. And at some point while they slept, she'd draped her leg over his lap. Her thigh rested over his cock, which was now harder than he ever remembered it being.

Fan-fucking-tastic.

All he really wanted to do was roll over and take her. To drive himself into her until everything around them faded away. He knew she'd be soft in all the right places and tight where it mattered most.

His heart nearly beat out of his chest at the thought. He already loved her mind and spirit, and now—finally holding her the way he'd always wanted to…

He ached from it, and the pressure of her thigh only made it worse. When a low growl rose from his throat as he tried to move, Lily's head popped up. Still sleepy, she peered up at him.

"Zach?"

"Shh, babe," he answered. "Everything's okay. Go back to sleep."

Without a word, she dropped her head to his shoulder and grabbed him tighter, wriggling a little to get settled back in.

Ah, fuck him. She'd shifted and situated her leg right over his cock again. Only this time, being awake, she had to have felt how hard he was.

She froze within his arms. Zach squeezed his eyes and bit back a curse.

Oh yeah, she felt it, all right.

Her hard swallow bumped against his left pecs, inches above a nipple that tightened on its own volition as her hand stilled on his abdomen. When she lifted her head again, he didn't know what he wanted to see on her face—horror or lust.

When he opened his eyes to meet hers, she was staring back at him with a hungry gaze, her lower lip caught between her teeth.

Seemed lust won out.

He didn't wait even a second to think about it—knowing if he did he'd only end up talking himself out of doing what he wanted most. So he cupped her cheek, tossed every bit of reasoning out the fucking window and kissed her.

Her lips were soft under his. Supple. And God, the way she kissed him back. His entire body sprang to life as his breaths became shallower. Quicker. But so were hers. She grabbed at his shirt, pulled him closer and opened her mouth to allow his tongue to explore inside.

He groaned—couldn't help it. She tasted like black-cherry wine and sleep mixed with a fiery passion. His new favorite flavor.

She pulled back and searched his eyes with hers. Confusion painted her expression, and he knew it only mirrored his own.

"Zach, what..."

"I don't know." *I don't care.* But even as he kissed her again, he knew. He knew in his heart she was meant to be his. Someway. Somehow.

She broke away from his mouth again, this time to push herself up and straddle his thighs. He ran his hands up into her hair. They both stilled. Panted.

"We can't do this... Can we? I shouldn't. We shouldn't. But *God*... Zach. What's going on here? I don't understand..." The words tumbled from her lips, even as she clutched his biceps and ground herself against him.

"What's to understand?" He pulled her closer, licked along the seam of her mouth until her body relaxed and she melted into him. The tiny, kitten-soft noises she made as she rubbed over him nearly killed him. Noises he drowned out with groans of his own.

"We're going to have to talk about this," she said when he moved his lips to her jawline. God, he loved the way her eyes drifted shut and her tongue peeked out to gloss her lower lip.

"Mm hmm." *Later.*

"Eric—"

"I know, babe," he interrupted, working his way down her neck with nips and licks.

"But—"

With absolutely no finesse, he traded positions with her, flipped her under him and covered her body with his. He needed to make her see, to make her trust in the here and now. "But nothing, Lil. You're here right now. With me."

"Zach..."

"Lil, babe. Talk to me. You know I'd never force you to do anything. But you have to help me out here. Tell me what *you* want."

She held his face in her hands and swirled her thumbs over his cheekbones. "I... I'm just not sure."

Yeah, he knew he was confusing the hell out of her right now. Still, he didn't want to give her the opportunity to say anything further, to possibly refuse what they both needed. In a cautious motion, he eased her t-shirt up her ribs and drew it over her head. "Could it be this maybe?"

As gently as he could, and despite the fire rushing through his veins, he silenced her next words by covering her mouth with his, then moved lower to breathe more featherlight kisses over her chest.

"Or this?"

He nuzzled the lace covering her nipple before closing his lips over the thin fabric and sucking on the tight bud. A sigh fell from her lips as she weaved her fingers through his hair.

When she arched into him, he slid one hand to the small of her back and the other between her shoulders to hold her there.

"Zach, you're killing me…"

"Never, love," he whispered against her breast. "I'm only helping you live."

He laid her back down and moved his lips lower, over the sexy dip of her tummy to rim her belly button with the tip of his tongue.

"I want… That's what I want. Help me, Zach. Help me live again."

She didn't have to ask him twice. He sat back on his heels and tugged his own shirt off before continuing his torturous meanderings down her stomach. With a firm grip he clutched her waist, yet hesitated to reach for the button on her jeans.

She bucked under him, and for a second he thought she may've changed her mind. But when he straightened his arms to hover over her and she dove for *his* fly, he tossed up a silent word of thanks to whatever god might be listening.

He rose to his knees, fished his wallet out of his pocket and dug through it for the condom he kept there, and then took over for her by pulling open his button-fly. When his jeans fell down his thighs, she looked him up and down and sucked in a shaky breath. His masculine pride roared at the underlying meaning.

Lily lifted her rear and tried to shove her own jeans past her hips, a difficult maneuver with him situated between her legs. "Hurry, Zach. God, I need this… I need you…"

He dropped the condom onto her belly, helped by lifting her legs and resting the backs of her calves upright against his chest. He curled his fingers under the waistband of her jeans, yanked and peeled them up and off, which left her legs raised like one of those sexy pin-up poses. He grabbed an ankle, kissed along the inside before nipping partway down her calf. She groaned, latched on to the back couch cushion and arched her delicate back once again. The action lifted her ass, and with one hand he held her there, rubbing against her slick heat with the head of his swollen cock.

It felt so good. *She* felt so good.

Pressure mounted inside his chest and traveled down into his balls. He hitched his chin and motioned to the condom. "Give me a hand and open that."

She did as he asked and handed over the ring of latex. With a firm grip still on her butt, he took the condom and reached between their bodies to cover himself. When she started to drop her legs, he stopped her with a deep-seated growl. "No, leave them up there. Put your feet on my shoulders."

She looked at him with a sexy hesitancy lighting her eyes.

"You've never been taken like this?" He leaned forward, aligning his cock and nudging her tight entrance. "Ah, babe. The angle..."

"Zach..."

He slipped inside her, just the head, but enough to make him catch his breath. "I can go so much deeper like this."

He gripped her hips, met her stare...and plunged deep. She cried out and turned her head into the pillow. He withdrew slowly—God, near torturously—only to thrust to the hilt once again.

So tight...goddamn it. He knew she would be. Her eyes flew open with his next drive into her. The passion swirling in them fit her, spoke volumes of who she was.

And—*fuck*—he wanted her to be his. Theirs.

She locked gazes with him, held onto him with her stare, with her spirit. He thrust again...and again...and again, losing a little more of himself with each one. When she tightened on him, he couldn't stand it any longer. He pushed her legs to each side and slid over her—harder into her—and took possession of her mouth. Their tongues sparred, dueled. She held him to her with fingers twisted in his hair, with her feet secure at the back of his thighs.

Holy shit…

She tilted her pelvis ever so slightly, and he felt it. Felt the little ripples as they morphed into tight contractions. With a primal groan, she broke away from their kiss as her sweet pussy clenched around his cock. The sensations assaulting him were too much, no way could he hold on, not for another second. He let go and soared with her, joined her in every wave.

"Oh dear God." Her heated breaths puffed against his shoulder on each word.

"Yeah," he blew against her neck. "No shit."

She pushed on his arm until he leaned up on his elbow and looked at her.

"Zach? What… Eric…"

The euphoric glow dancing just a few moments ago in her eyes was quickly turning into gut-wrenching alarm. He couldn't let that happen. If it did, if she withdrew from him…

No.

"Lily, easy now—"

"God, explain this to me. Please. I don't understand…" She pinned him with a stare that bulldozed straight past alarm and ended up somewhere in the vicinity of panic.

"Babe, it's okay. We'll figure it out. Together."

"Together," she echoed, with a quiet disbelief in her voice. "I never knew. You were always right there, too… But I never knew…"

He smiled and nuzzled her cheek in an attempt to reassure her. "I know."

She wrapped her arms around his shoulders and buried her face into his neck. "Oh, Zach. What in the hell am I going to do?"

Chapter Three

Eighteen months.

Well, really eighteen months, two weeks and three days.

And nine godforsaken hours.

That's how long he'd been gone. Too long, too much time. Time enough for people to change, for *her* to change.

Lily blew out a long, anxious breath.

Eric—in all his six-foot-two, blond-haired, blue-eyed, red-white-and-blue-American-pride powerhouse glory—ambled into the small reception hall and tossed his dusty duffle bag next to the door. He wore the standard beige Desert Camouflage Uniform and beat-to-hell work boots that every other Marine did, the shade so reminiscent of the bland tans of Mother Earth and the rare mud of the region where he'd spent the last year and a half.

But, Lord have mercy, how he filled them out.

His folks had picked him up from the airport and driven him straight over. Within seconds of him entering the small room, extended family, friends and neighbors, not to mention all the tough-ass guys he'd served with in the Chicago Police Department, surrounded him with bear hugs, hefty claps on the back and steady pumps of handshakes. A few of his buddies even threw in a good-natured whack or two upside the head.

Their man had finally come home.

The deep, whispered voice at the edge of her ear rattled her nerves even further.

"Damn, Lil. He looks great."

She tamped down the annoying belly-flutters and nodded. Swallowing past the Texas-sized knot in her throat, she tried to breathe through the sudden painful tightness binding her chest while fresh tears stung her eyes. "Yeah. He does." *Too good, in fact.*

"You scared?"

Lord, and how. "Terrified."

Zach rubbed tiny little circles at the small of her back, but his attempt at reassurance did little to dissuade her ever-increasing nervousness.

"Not to worry, sugar. It's still Eric. He's the same, no matter how long he's been gone."

She clutched her entwined fingers against the steady beat crashing inside her chest, all the while knowing that if she wasn't even close to being the same person she was before he left, how could Eric be? "I don't know, Zach. I think we've all probably changed even more than we realize."

He tensed ever so slightly behind her. "You've got nothing to worry about, you know. Any issues he'll have with this will fall on me. After all, I'm the one he asked to watch over you while he was gone."

She bit back a distraught chuckle before it turned into a pitiful cry. "Somehow, I don't think what happened was exactly what he meant by *'Watch over her.'*"

His soothing hand continued to swirl its wicked magic on her lower back, then searched even lower along the swell of her hip.

"Come on, you know Eric's like a brother to me. We'll work it out, just like we talked about, I promise. We'll make him see. Have a little patience."

She softened a bit against the tingles that plagued her insides, the sensation a heady mixture of fear commingled with utter hope.

"Oh, Zach… It's been so long…" Seeing Eric again after so long just brought back all the heartache from when he left. The hurt, the shock of him not wanting her to wait for him.

She thought he loved the excitement, the freshness of their budding passion. The newness of their relationship was something she had cherished, something she believed Eric had shared with her. To realize maybe he hadn't…

"God, I keep going back to when he told me not to wait for him… Maybe he doesn't even want me anymore. Maybe he won't—"

"He does," Zach's breathy statement interrupted, "He'd be insane not to, Lil. You have to trust that."

She attempted a cheerful smile at Zach's optimistic words, but she knew the uneasy twitch of her lips appeared more forlorn than anything else. How did he do that? The way he always knew what to say, the way he understood exactly what she needed—she so loved that about him.

When Eric found her from the opposite side of the hall, she stiffened. At that moment she knew what he thought, that she'd waited for him. And she had…but there was so much more to it than that.

God, how was she going to explain all this?

Eric studied her for a moment before his lips curled slightly upward, his oh-so-devilish dimple breaking the smooth skin of his right cheek. The heat in his eyes pinned her to where she stood. She wouldn't have been able to move even if she wanted to.

He looked then to Zach—her personal tower of strength who stood mere inches behind her—only to return his searing gaze to her once again. The blue ice of his intense stare cut into her soul from clear across the room. Fear of what might come next—of failing to get what she now realized she wanted more than anything—made her nearly run away and hide. But she stood firm and stomped down her misgivings. She wanted *him*, more than she wanted to give in to all the what-if's and maybe's.

"This is it, babe. Go easy, just like we talked about," Zach whispered against her ear.

The heat of his breath sent a shiver to the most sensitive depths of her body. Yeah, they'd discussed what to do months ago, how they'd explain and make Eric understand, hopefully even accept. It all came down to this, to what happened right now.

Steady as she-fricking-goes.

Her nerves were having a free-for-all. She treasured both men—so much so she'd never feel whole without them. They completed her. *Both* of them. She knew that now, beyond a shadow of doubt.

As her stomach quivered and her heart clenched, she took the first step toward what she hoped would be her future. What had to be her future. Nothing less would do. Not for her, anyway.

Not for any of them.

Lily.

There stood Lily.

Fresh. Sun-kissed. Not to mention drop-dead sexy.

And behind her stood Zach, the man he thought of as a brother more times than he could count.

But he couldn't keep his eyes off the supple woman in front of his best friend. That she was here… God, he almost couldn't believe it. She'd waited for him, even after he'd told her not to. Relief burst in his chest, a heated flash of desire exploded everywhere else.

Damn, she looked so nervous. But she shouldn't be. He was home now, done for good. Even Uncle Sam couldn't drag him back again. He'd served honorably and with everything he had in him, gave himself over fully to every intense moment of his sworn duty.

But now, time was his.

Hers.

Theirs.

He smiled tightly through the last of the welcoming handshakes and hugs. His family had insisted on throwing him this little shindig. A coming home, of sorts. They were thrilled to have him back, in one piece. Alive and uninjured. Well, physically anyway.

They wanted to celebrate and he couldn't deny them that. He wanted to as well, for more than one reason now.

The edge of his lip twitched and blood rushed like fire through his veins. He knew the charge was from seeing Lily again, but the sensations were so close to that all-too-familiar panic, the memorable, undeniable fear…

Fuck…

Even through any happiness he may feel, darkness always lurked close by. He cursed the war-torn shit that chose that exact moment to pop in his head. The memories always attacked him at such inopportune times. Times like now.

He was so tired of consciously pushing away all those fucked-up, morose thoughts of what happened on the other side of the planet. But after months of living the nightmare, he'd become a master at masking—thank God. An instant flick of an internal switch, and presto…the shit disappeared. Unfortunately, it never stayed away nearly long enough.

With all the aggravating memories temporarily forced out of his head, he concentrated on the heavenly woman gliding toward him now.

Perfect. Incredible. And—holy Christ—his. He hoped. Thoughts of the hurt he caused her when he left invaded his mind and he nearly cringed.

But, still…she was here now. What else could that possibly mean?

The small crowd parted as she drew near. Her tear-brightened smile lit up the room, her choke on a half-laugh, half-sob as she came closer convinced him to stifle one of his own.

Lily.

She drifted into his arms, silent. He latched onto her delicate body so tight, stroked over and over the long, dark curls that fell well past her shoulders. Man, how he missed the smell of her shampoo, the clean fragrance of her lavender soap he remembered so well. He'd thought back often, while huddled in some dark alley or burned-out building, of that exact scent. Of how he'd wrapped his hand in her hair and breathed in her perfect aroma as he came hard inside her heat.

Her power—that brilliant clarity she radiated—attacked him in a big way. He closed his eyes, buried his face into her hair while he sucked her essence in deep. The lushness of her curves snuggled up against the hard exterior of his tight, trained body.

No way could she be more of a godsend. She felt like pure, unadulterated heaven.

"You smell so good, sweetheart." He groaned and drew in a deep breath. "Lavender, Lil. My favorite."

Her sigh blew hot and heavy against the sensitive skin of his neck. "I know. Oh, Eric…"

"Shh, babe. S'all cool. I'm here. I'm home now, Lil. For good."

She pulled back, the tenderness of her gentle fingers on his cheek a more than welcome touch. When she stood on her toes to kiss him, aligned her perfect lips with his, every muscle in his body slackened and he felt blessed with a calm he'd not experienced in well over a year.

The peck of her lips was gentle. Soft. Shy.

And too damn short.

"For good?" she repeated against his mouth.

"Yeah," he breathed. "I'm done."

She nodded, apparently satisfied with his answer, and twisted to lay her head on his shoulder. Then Zach appeared on his other side, ready to grip him in one of those macho-man half-hugs, complete with the required slap on the shoulder. The gesture meant the world to him.

"Damn, I'm glad you're home, Eric. You don't look any worse for the wear either, man."

Eric smiled. The action made his face feel funny since he hadn't smiled for real in what seemed like ages. "Nah, not too much."

Not on the outside, anyway.

"What d'ya say to a beer? You look like a man who could use a cold one."

"Yeah, damn straight."

Christ, he needed this. Normalcy. Good ol' everyday shit. No more duck and run, no more fifteen minute battle naps, the end to war zones and ready-to-eat meals in shitty throwaway packages. And the end to daily dealings with death.

But what he really needed right now more than anything was Lily. To pick up from where they left off, or start over new again. Hell, either way, it didn't matter to him. As long as he could be with her, buried inside her, he'd be cool. Better than cool. He'd be back on his way to whole again. Back on his way to being the man he was before, when he'd been lucky enough to have those few weeks with her.

Weeks he'd wasted by not making love to her every chance he got—a regret he couldn't wait to rectify now.

In the deep crevices of his mind, he knew now that he'd been counting on the fact he and Lily had something together. Something strong, worth waiting for. He sometimes wondered—when he allowed himself those rare moments of self-reflection—where the strength to tell her not to wait for him had come from. But he had to do it, had to draw on that courage from deep inside his soul. War was unpredictable at best, and he hated to think of her heart broken any worse than it already would be should he meet the same unfortunate end so many of his Marine brethren had. At the time, he thought he was doing the right thing by her. Saving her from potential heartbreak. But now? Now he was just so stoked that she hadn't listened to him.

Not once in eighteen months had he ever stopped thinking about her, ever stopped loving her.

He held her now, her softness nestled snug against his side. Christ, he couldn't wait to get her alone. To get his mouth on her, to get inside her.

He secured an arm around her waist and together they headed to a table near the bar. Zach slapped a cold longneck in his free hand, handed one to Lily and they all clanked their bottles together as the crowd around them lifted their own.

"Here's to you. Welcome home, my friend," Zach called out.

A chorus of "Hell, yeah", "'Bout time" and whistles and shouts rang throughout the room. Eric leaned down to touch his lips to Lily's. Oh man, she tasted so good. So perfect.

She pulled away far too fast, worked her lips between her teeth and flushed a crimson red before flashing a quick peek to Zach. Eric caught the glance, along with the obvious connection the two shared for the fraction of a second they each held the other's gaze. Right then his world blew apart with an invisible punch dead center to his gut.

Well, well…

I'll be a son of a bitch.

Chapter Four

As the party wound down, Lily's nerves ratcheted up. Eric had seen the sudden look she threw at Zach. She wanted to kick herself seven ways to Sunday for such a stupid show of her overwhelming emotions. Since then, pain—combined with a fair amount of anger—flowed from Eric with a palpable restraint.

God, she didn't want to hurt him. She loved him. Loved them both. They already consumed such a huge chunk of her heart it ached. Now, all she wanted was them in her life—and in her bed. Forever.

Would Eric agree? Would he even understand?

A few hours later, all the food had been eaten, the welcome-home cake had been cut and devoured and the goodbyes were at last said. The three of them were the only ones remaining in the quiet banquet hall.

Eric ran a hand over his shorn hair. "I think I'll head to my folk's. Tonight's been—" Pain lit his eyes again. "Eye-opening," he finally finished.

An unwelcome tingle bloomed in the center of her chest. "No, wait. Don't go just yet. Let's… Come on, let's go back to my place. We'll talk some more, hang out. Like old times. Okay?"

When he didn't answer, she added an earnest, "Please, Eric."

After a moment he nodded, his anger a blatant force. "Sure thing, Lil. A talk right about now might be good. But only if he comes along, too."

Zach looked up from tearing the soggy label off his bottle of Bud. "Me?"

Eric lifted his rock-hard body off the small wooden chair. "Yeah. You. It's funny, but I got the damndest feeling the two of you have something to tell me."

She wrung her hands in her lap and stared at him. What was she supposed to say? Oh, yeah, by the way, I slept with Zach while you were overseas. But it's really not what you think, Eric. I want you, I want you both.

Sure, that'd go over so damn well right now.

No. She needed to approach this like she and Zach had planned. Slow and easy, warm him to the notion the three of them belonged together.

They rode in silence the entire fifteen-minute trip to her house. Settled between Zach in the driver's seat and Eric on the passenger side of Zach's pickup, she almost blew an internal gasket at the tension radiating inside the small cab. But no matter how pissed he was, Eric still held out his hand to help her from the truck once they arrived at her house. She cherished that about him, how considerate, caring and tenderly he always treated her.

The unexpected gesture brought to mind the perfect evening they'd spent together, a month or so before he'd left.

Their first kiss.

It had come straight out of the blue. After attending a concert at a local theater, they'd decided to take a walk together through the freshly fallen snow. Heading toward the deserted Riverwalk, quiet and comfortable in each other's company, he'd suddenly stopped her with a gentle hand on her elbow. And just like that, he lowered his lips to hers. God, it was a moment she'd never forget.

Somehow at the same time, though, she'd been riddled with confusion—over Zach. She never really understood why, not until she'd spent that night with him. It was then all her jumbled emotions came into sharp focus.

An ah-ha moment if ever there was one.

She pushed the key into the doorknob, unlocked her front door and entered the little bungalow ahead of them. After she flicked on the lamp next to the closet, she tossed her purse and coat on the couch and went straight for the kitchen. Liquid encouragement was an absolute must at this point.

Eric and Zach hovered shoulder to shoulder just inside the kitchen doorway.

"Three glasses?" she asked, fingers wrapped around the neck of an unopened bottle of Jack.

"Sure," Zach said.

"Yeah," Eric added.

With the kitchen island the only barrier separating her from the two hard men, she tossed a few ice cubes into three rocks glasses and poured. The deep, amber liquid shimmered in each glass against the dim light above her stove.

After she sucked back her share, she poured another finger worth, and pounded that one just as quickly before setting her glass in the sink. Her body itched; she was scared and excited at the same time. She expected what came next, and honestly, was surprised it hadn't come any sooner.

"So, Zach, how long you been fucking her?"

Eric's tone held a shitload of emotion. His free hand fisted and flexed at his side. The hurt, the anger had him completely riled as he rocked back on his heels.

She really couldn't blame him.

Zach coughed on a sip of the Jack. A lock of chin-length, chestnut-brown hair fell across his cheek. He tucked the stray strands behind his ear and sucked back a clean breath before he answered. "Shit, Eric. Way to get to the heart of it."

Eric shrugged on another swallow and shoved his fist deep into the pants pocket of his DCU pants. "I see no particular reason to beat around the damn bush. So when?

Was I even on the plane yet? Did you at least wait until I left the fucking country?"

"Eric," she whispered. Pleaded.

He plastered her with an indignant stare. "Don't, Lil. Don't deny it. It insults me. I'm not stupid. I saw you. Saw the way you looked at him." Hurt passed in a dark cloud over his face. "Why the two of you? I just want to fucking know why."

She averted her eyes and concentrated on the ice in Eric's glass instead. Cool, it reminded her to be cool. "It wasn't like that, Eric. Not at all."

"But you are fucking him, right? Tell me I'm not wrong on that account, Lil. Tell me I'm not that goddamn blind."

She lifted her head and confronted his stare with an air of defensiveness. "No. You're not wrong. Is that what you want to hear? Do you want to hear that since you were gone, I simply moved on to the next available man? That I fucked Zach because you weren't around?"

Eric's stance stiffened. The way he leaned forward in primal battle-readiness had her regretting those last words.

Sometimes he piqued her like nobody else could. But that was still no excuse for harshness. She needed to tone herself down right now, or the entire situation would disintegrate beyond repair in the span of a heartbeat.

She softened, and chose her next words more carefully. "Because if I told you that, I'd be lying. Yes, Eric, I slept with Zach. One time." She closed her eyes to keep the tears that threatened at bay. "It was just...just something that happened. We didn't plan it. God... I was hurting, and...and he was there for me."

Oh, the way Zach had held her that night. So comforting, so sincere. And then afterwards when they'd woken in each other's arms... He knew what she needed, had given her the solace she'd craved ever since Eric had left. Neither one of them intended for the evening to end up the way it did.

She opened her eyes and cut her stare into Eric as far as it would go. "But you were, too. In my mind, you were with us."

Eric's face flushed. "Bullshit."

"No!" She shook her head, desperate for him to understand, but worried she was failing at it miserably. "Ask him. Turn to your best friend and ask him who else we talked about. Ask him who else was with the two of us that night."

Her heart pounded while Eric's head dropped.

Was she pushing too hard? Lord, how the tension radiated off him. She could feel his weariness, the way he rode the fine line along a sharp razor's edge.

And yet she had to push further.

"Ask him."

Instead, Eric spun and stalked from the kitchen. He made his way into her small living room, his big body a major presence when he landed on her small flowered couch.

She followed and stood in front of him, the coffee table between them.

"Eric."

Head hung, he ignored her.

"Eric, please."

Zach came behind her and curled his large hand over her shoulder. She sucked in the strength he offered and went for it.

"Say something. Anything. Tell me to fuck off. Tell me..." Her voice cracked and she had to stop a moment to collect herself before she could continue. "Oh, Eric, just tell me you still want me."

He lifted his head then. The hurt and anguish on his face wrenched at her stomach.

"I dreamed of you. Did you know that? Every damn night. During the day, too. Bombs exploded, I saw you. Men died in my arms, I saw you. Women were huddled over their children in the filthy corners of the streets, and I fucking saw you. You never left my thoughts. You never left my heart. And

I come home to…to…" He sucked in a breath as fire lit the dark depths of his eyes. "When I saw you tonight, I figured you'd waited for me. That we could pick up from where we left off. That's all I really wanted. All I'd waited months to find out. But shit, Lil. How could you come to me like that tonight after you've been in my *best friend's* arms?"

She swallowed around the all-too-familiar lump, her lips and fingertips alight with the tingle of raw nerves. "But it wasn't like that. You were with me, too. Every day. In my mind, in my heart. And Zach's, too."

Righteous anger etched the hard planes of his face.

"Zach?" He pummeled his best friend with an icy stare. "Yeah, Zach, why don't you tell me how I was in your thoughts while you were fucking her? Enlighten me, please. Because, Christ, I can't even imagine it."

Zach spoke then, the lone voice of reason in a sea of tumultuous emotion. "Okay, everyone hold up here a second. I think we all need to take a step back—"

Eric nodded and blew out a sardonic chuckle with another swipe of his hand over his head. "Yeah. Let's all just hold up and soak that in a minute, why don't we? What a perfect fucking thing to dwell on."

Lily wanted to crawl in a hole. She hadn't known exactly what to expect once they arrived at her place, but this certainly wasn't what she pictured happening. Not by a long shot.

Their deep breaths rasped in the sudden uncomfortable silence. A hefty amount of fear coiled in her gut. She was blowing this, she just knew it. Yes, she wanted the three of them to be together. But like this? With Eric's anger so apparent? So raw? Apprehension warred with a flare of heat low in her belly. She didn't want the panic to win, but at the same time, she couldn't deny it any longer either.

Eric looked menacing. Coiled muscles flexed past his rolled up sleeves; thick, ropy veins jutted from under his skin.

Antagonism seeped from every pore with such evident strength. God, it killed her to see him in such pain.

She didn't want him to be like this. She didn't want him hurt and pissed.

She only wanted to love him.

He shot to his feet. "I need to go."

"Wait..." She lurched from Zach's grip. *No, no, no!* "Stay. We have to—"

"Talking's overrated, babe," he interrupted as if he read her mind. "I gotta bounce. Get out of here before I say or do something I'll regret later."

She stilled. Her lungs seized with desperation. "Eric, please. Don't leave angry. Just... God, don't leave."

Don't leave angry?

Hell, his anger was the last piece of sanity he had. He held on to it with a ferocious grip, that final thread to reality blowing in a hurricane of gale-force emotions. The rational soldier inside him, however, knew he needed to take that proverbial step back and rein it in before he exploded. But he didn't have the wherewithal to actually do that quite yet. Not when it came to this.

Not when it came to his Lily.

In reality, her confession shouldn't have been much of a surprise. After all, he'd *told* her not to wait for him. He'd left it hanging like that, with her in tears and him telling her to move on. But deep down he assumed—prayed—she'd be there, waiting for him when he got back. Assumed she'd want him as much as he ever wanted her.

Apparently, he was way off base.

Fuck, I'm such an ass.

He reluctantly sat again, fought to control the impulse to smash Zach's face in and sucked a breath in deep. He rested his elbows on the top of his thighs.

"Sorry, babe. Anger's all I have left. Take it or leave it." He looked past the ice in the glass held in his hands to the dirty boots laced up his ankles. He felt like shit. Complete, utter shit. But he didn't care. He just didn't have the ability to in him anymore.

In his periphery, Zach wrapped his arm across Lily's shoulders and squeezed her back against his chest. "Maybe now isn't the time for this." He spoke low, right next to her ear, but Eric heard him anyway, clear as day.

Seeing the two of them together, with a closeness that went beyond their physical bodies, burned him. He thought back to all the times the three of them had hung out before he shipped off and, hell, even before then. The easiness the two held toward each other should've spoken just as loud as Zach telling him—on more than one occasion throughout the years—"how great she is". He should've known Zach had wanted her. But he'd ignored any feelings of—what? jealousy? possessiveness?—simply because they'd all been close friends for so damn long. She fit in with them so well, been the lush softness between the hard and rough edges that made up him and Zach.

He'd always wanted her, so he supposed it made sense that Zach would, too.

Why hadn't he seen this coming?

"What the hell do you want from me?" He had to know. She'd gone on and on about how he'd been in her thoughts, been with them both. How could that be? How could she sleep with Zach and think of him at the same time? It didn't make any sense. The idea was too much to wrap his weary brain around.

She left Zach's hold and came to sit in front of him on the coffee table. He clenched his jaw when their knees touched, when her luscious lavender scent drifted under his nose. Christ, he still wanted her. So damn much. That desire had never gone away.

She took his glass of whiskey and set it to the side, then slipped her hands into his and hung them between his knees, fingers entwined. Behind her, Zach widened his stance and folded his arms over his chest. His expression was difficult to read, but Eric could sense he held back with an edge of wariness.

"What I want," she started, "is you. That's never changed."

He blew out a skeptical chuckle, but couldn't quite keep his pathetic heart from quickening its pace. "Me? Really? How's that, babe? How is it you want me, when you've already got Zach?"

She worked her lips between her teeth in that telltale little way she had and tossed a look over her shoulder to Zach before coming back at him. "You see…that's just it, Eric.

"I want him, too."

Chapter Five

Zach hung back and contemplated the scene playing out in front of him. Usually it took a lot to surprise Eric, and Lil had certainly done a great job of it just now. He felt for the guy, he really did. But when it came to Lily and what she wanted, Zach found himself helpless to resist. And it would only be a matter of time before Eric would be, too.

For all Zach knew, maybe he already was.

He'd wanted to cringe before, when she told Eric to ask him who else had been with them the one night they'd spent together. But he also knew she didn't say it to hurt him. Eric had always been in her heart, always would be. He and Lily had talked so much about what they meant to each other over the last few months. He stopped doubting her feelings for him a while ago.

She loved him.

But she loved Eric, too.

And it felt right. He didn't know why, but it did. Normally, jealousy would eat away at him. And if this had been any other relationship, any other woman, he'd probably kill another man who would try to come close to what was his.

But Lily was different. Special. With a free spirit too wild to tame, she simply glowed. His perfect Lily. She lived fire and ice, breathed pure passion and pleasure. And he couldn't wait to see that fire and passion multiply and blaze inside her. To feel it.

Back in his senior year of college, he'd witnessed firsthand how a woman reacted when two men made love to her. Now older and more experienced, he wanted nothing more than to see Lily in that light. For him and Eric to bring her higher than she'd ever been.

Lily had told him after they were together that night months ago, it'd be a one-time thing. Couldn't be repeated. Not without Eric. He respected her wishes, but God, he ached for her too. He wanted this just as much as she did.

"Both of us?" Eric finally managed.

The poor bastard was stunned stupid. Without a doubt, this couldn't be what he expected. Hell, why would he?

"You're kidding, right? What the…" Eric turned to him then, and Zach could almost picture the light bulb going off over his head. "Oh, *Christ*."

Eric hung his head, and then lifted it a second later with an edge of revelation in his eyes as he peered at Lily. "He told you, didn't he?"

Yeah, he had. Lying on the couch after they made love, they'd ended up talking for hours. Every subject was broached, including past relationships. At first he'd hesitated to say anything, but something inside him couldn't help but want to nudge her thoughts along. So he confessed it was he and Eric who had been with the woman back in college. Eric had visited him on campus while on leave during his first tour of duty. After a long night of pool, darts and way too much beer, they'd drunkenly shared a one night stand with a more than willing co-ed. The tryst wasn't one of his more stellar moments, but the raw pleasure he'd received that night stuck with him to this day.

"Lil, that happened ages ago. I'm not that kid anymore. This isn't a joke to me. And it's not a one-night-stand either. You mean so much more to me than that—"

"Hold on just a sec." She straightened her back. "I'm not a kid here either, Eric. I know what I want. You. And Zach. I'm being honest with you about that."

Eric flopped back on the couch. "Fuck," he muttered.

Zach moved then to sit behind Lily on the coffee table. He straddled her, wrapped his arms around her waist and tucked her thighs between his as she continued to hold Eric's hands. She trembled in his arms. The telling reaction clawed at his control.

"*Fuck,*" Eric groaned again and blasted him with a stare. "How can we… You're cool with this?"

Zach released her waist and smoothed his hands up and down Lily's arms with firm, even strokes. Goosebumps rose under his touch and the quick pace of her heart beat hard against his chest. God, he'd do just about anything to take her anxiety away.

"Yeah, I am. What can I say? The woman knows what she wants. And I happen to feel pretty damn lucky I'm a part of that. She fits with us, Eric. You know she does. You've known it for years."

Eric closed his eyes. "I… *Shit.* You're both asking a lot from me right now. I'm not who I used to be. I'm not the same man anymore."

Zach couldn't begin to understand the demons that raged inside his best friend's head. But he knew one thing for certain—Eric loved Lily. The question was, could he bring himself to share her? To share her love in return?

"I know you're not the same. I never expected you to be." Lily lifted one of his hands to her lips and kissed each knuckle. "Let's just have tonight, then. Let me calm your anger, quiet your pain. All you have to do is feel. Just feel me, Eric."

Zach winced a little inside. He knew she craved them both, but damn it… He'd told her months ago they'd need to ease Eric into this, into what she wanted. Into what they both wanted. If she pushed too hard, moved too fast…

Eric opened his eyes and Zach immediately sympathized with the ocean of angry pain swirling in his stare. He was torn, and Zach related to that. Eric could be a hard, difficult man. But Zach also knew he loved the way a woman looked and felt at the height of her pleasure. Soft and supple, her delicate back arched as she found her bliss, her pouty mouth barely open in a moan of ecstasy. A picture of pure, erotic love.

And in the most elemental terms, that was what this was about. Lily and her pleasure. Her complete love and contentment. As a direct result of hers, they'd have their own, and on a much higher plane than the mere physical. Protectiveness, nurturing, and trust would be ingrained within them. They'd wrap her in a tight cocoon of all that, and Zach knew that after a while, they'd never be able to walk away from her or the natural high they'd both get from pleasing and sating her every desire.

He watched Eric with quiet patience as an internal struggle battled within his friend's expression, and waited along with Lily for the answer that could possibly change the rest of their lives.

He sure as hell never expected the one they got.

"I can't."

Two words never crushed Lily more.

"What? You can't?" The echo fell from suddenly numb lips.

Eric stared at their entwined hands, gave a squeeze then let go. Her heart once again shattered into a thousand tiny shards that splintered throughout her body.

"No." He stood, brushed past her knees, and strode closer to the door. "I'm jumping out of my skin here. All I want to do right now is kick his ass," he motioned to Zach with a hitch of his chin and a steely glare, "and then take you to bed and stay there for a week. Hell, a month. But I can't do either one of those things. Not without losing myself somewhere along the way. And that I won't do." He seared her with a stare. "Not even for you, Lil."

And then he did the one thing she never anticipated. He turned his back on her—just spun right around—and waltzed out the front door.

She froze between Zach's legs and stared at the closed door. A long moment and a deep breath later, she whispered, "He left."

God, her heart was being ripped from her chest.

Zach rested his cheek against the crown of her head. "Yeah. He did."

She swallowed back a desperate moan. Her eyes welled and her vision blurred with unshed tears. "You told me he'd want this too."

Strong fingers wrapped around her upper arms in a tight grip while his thumbs massaged along her triceps. "I know, baby."

She scooted forward and pierced him with an incensed stare over her shoulder, the tears momentarily forgotten. "*'I know?'* All you can say is 'I know'?"

"He's on edge, Lil. Cut him some slack. I told you this may take a while, to move slow."

"I thought I was going slow. God, Zach." She buried her face in her hands and fought renewed tears. "He left me."

Zach wrapped his arms around her. "No. He didn't. Not really. Give him some space. A little time."

"Time?" She couldn't keep the anguish from poisoning her voice. "I've run out of time. *We've* run out of time."

"Lil…"

She whirled from his arms and stood to face him. "Don't 'Lil' me. Just…don't." She swatted at an errant tear that finally fell down her cheek. "I've waited so long for…for both of you… I can't… Oh, Zach." She drew in a shaky breath. "It's not just that. You saw him. He needs us, too. So much. I can't stand to see him like this. Hurt. Angry. We can help him work through his pain, be with him when he needs us. I just... I know we can. We can do this, make it better, together."

Zach slid off the table, stood, and opened his arms. "Come here."

She couldn't help it, she rushed back into his hold. Oh God, he felt so good. Strong arms wrapped around her, reassuring hands stroked her back. Her one night with him had started this way, with his caring and gentle caresses. For a six-foot-one bruiser, he had so much compassion, held such tenderness.

When Zach had first told her of his and Eric's one-time ménage a trois, she'd been...hurt really wasn't the right word for it. Shocked, maybe. It wasn't as if sharing lovers was something she'd ever considered before, at least not back then. But they'd done it. Eric and Zach...and they'd done it with someone else. The instant flare of jealousy when he announced his secret shook her. She shouldn't have given in to the envy, but in a small way she had. Since they'd all been friends for what seemed like forever, she'd always thought of the men as belonging only to her. Three peas nestled together in a cozy pod.

Sure, when she and Zach had been in college and Eric had been stationed out of state during his first tour, they'd lost touch, gone a couple months here or there without a call or email, or stopping in to see each other whenever they were home. But ever since she and Zach graduated college and Eric had come home after his first deployment, they'd been inseparable.

And that's when the confusion had hit. Both men had matured so much while the three had been apart. The new emotions she faced toward them scared her, but astounded her at the same time. They were strong—and sometimes surprisingly erotic—and they only served to confuse the hell out of her. She'd struggled within her own mind and decided it would be best to push the wayward feelings aside. The last thing she'd wanted was to mess up her friendship with these guys. They meant too much for her to do that.

So, they'd gone on that way, year after year. Being best friends and doing all the things close friends do. Movies, parties, dancing and dinners out. Nothing out of the ordinary, nothing that would remotely tip the scales.

Then Eric had kissed her after the concert that night, and everything changed.

But regardless, what still amazed her was the fact she hadn't been able to make sense of all those muddled feelings she held inside toward the two men. Not until her night with Zach and his little confession. She knew at that point nothing less than having them both in her life would make her happy.

She needed them. She felt whole with them. Zach understood.

Why couldn't Eric?

Tears flowed in fitful waves, soaking a dark stain into the front of Zach's olive green t-shirt.

"Take it easy, baby. He'll be back. I know for a fact he won't be able to stay away. Not from you. Not from this."

She sniffled and calmed some, then raised her head. "How do you know? What if he's never okay with this? With me? God, Zach, I've made such a mess of things."

With a more than easy touch, he cupped her cheeks in his palms. "No, you haven't. I wouldn't be here if I didn't want this, Lil. And as for Eric... He's got to be in shock right now. This couldn't have been what he expected when he flew off that base this morning. I'm sure he figured he'd come home to a small party, get more than a little wasted and end up back here in bed with you. We had to have thrown him for a serious loop."

She made a weak attempt at a reassuring smile as he lifted his thumbs to wipe away her tears. Tension flowed out of her shoulders. "You're right. I just know how amazing we've always been together, the three of us. How perfect this can be. I want him to see that..."

He brushed his lips over hers. So gentle. So simple.

"He will. He'll be back. Then you'll have us. Both of us."

Butterflies raced in her stomach, heat pooled between her thighs. And at that moment, a sweet yearning slowly overtook her sorrow.

The promise she made to herself that she wouldn't be with either man separately weighed heavy now. But even despite her personal pledge, she reacted to Zach—not only to his encouraging words, but to the gentle man holding her so tenderly in his arms.

She wanted him. Needed him.

But at the same time she ached to her bones for Eric.

Their gazes held for a long moment. Caught up in the calm he exuded, she rose to her toes and pressed her lips against Zach's. She needed some semblance of peace, just a little to still her rambunctious thoughts. Craving his serenity more than anything, she found herself greedily taking what he offered, any repercussions be damned.

Zach bent his knees, wound his arms around her lower back and lifted her closer to deepen the kiss. Heat radiated from his body, his erection pressed low on her belly.

And she was right there with him. Her lips parted to accept his wicked tongue, her mind whirled as she clutched his shoulders tighter.

Then a vision of Eric flashed behind her closed eyes.

Oh, God, I shouldn't be doing this... It's not fair...

The instant the thought burst through her mind, the front door shot open.

"Zach, I need the keys for your truck..."

She tore away from Zach's kiss and spun within his arms. Eric stood in the doorway, one hand held in a death grip on the doorknob, the other clutched onto the jamb. He looked her up and down as his face flushed red and fury lit his eyes. But if she wasn't mistaken, there was more to that intent look of his. Desire? Could that be what she saw?

Her heart raced at the notion. Did he still want her? Had he changed his mind about what she and Zach offered?

No. That couldn't be. It was only her wishful imagination taking over the shame from getting caught doing what she said she'd *never* do. Besides, Eric had made his stance perfectly clear earlier when he walked out on them.

He didn't want her.

But that look… The raw sexual power pulsing from his body was undeniable.

"Eric… It's not…"

"I see you wasted no time, *babe*."

Zach stormed forward then, pushed her behind him in a protective gesture. Ire of his own etched the hard planes of his face. "Shut the fuck up, Eric. You don't have a damn clue what's going on here."

"Don't I?" Eric stalked further into the living room, more than primed and ready for a fight. "Seems pretty fucking obvious to me."

Zach got right up into Eric's face. They stood nose to nose, both of them seething. "No. It's not. Maybe you really are a goddamn blind man."

All the blood rushed from Lily's head and settled into a cold ball in the center of her stomach. Christ, they were going to come to blows if she didn't do something fast.

Several options flew through her mind on how she might stop them. She could jump between their hulking bodies and hope to hell she didn't get caught in the middle of a bloody fistfight. Or she could take matters into her own hands and try to distract them.

Her mind sparked with sudden hope.

This could be it… And if she handled it right—forced the issue, so to speak—the high-strung emotional turn the entire night had taken could end up being so worth it.

Oh, hell yeah. The latter seemed like a much better plan.

Chapter Six

Eric never wanted to slam his fist into another human being's face so much in his life. With his hand already bunched at his side, he was ready to make the first move and take Zach out. But then, in his periphery, Lily stepped back. The action distracted him and her deep sigh dragged his attention past Zach and into her direction.

One simple look at her precious face and he fucking lost it. Christ, he was so gone.

She grabbed the hem of her tight little t-shirt and wriggled it over her head. Chestnut-brown curls fell around her bare shoulders in the wake. The lace of her black bra barely covered those perfect, dark pink nipples of hers. The soft mounds of her golden-tanned breasts rose, and then dipped into a blissful valley of heart-stopping cleavage.

By the time she reached a hand to the back hook of the bra, Zach had spun around and appeared just as entranced as he found himself.

Fuck, she so didn't fight fair.

"What the hell are you doing?" He growled the words on a step away from Zach.

A sultry lowering of her eyelashes and a bite to her bottom lip led to a throaty, "Hopefully stopping a bloodbath."

Eric flashed a glance to Zach, who blew out a breath, folded his arms over his chest, then hung and shook his head. Eric could've sworn he bit back a curse.

He returned his interest to the wicked seductress before him. "I'm not in the mood for games here, Lil."

She left the clasp of her bra closed and brought her hands around to her stomach instead. The way she teased her own skin with those delicate fingers of hers had him rock hard in an instant.

God, he should be pissed—and he was—but his body reacted so strongly to her, too. Always had. He could never deny the effect she had on him—physical or otherwise.

"No games, Eric. Not a single one. I told you before, I know what I want."

His mind reeled, his blood burned.

"I want you." A predatory step. "I want Zach." Another seductive step.

The rise and fall of her still-covered breasts on every word, along with the movement of her fingers as they traveled higher to skim over them, tore him up. Could he do this? Could he give her what she wanted and not lose himself at the same time?

He honestly didn't know if he could share her. Didn't know if he wanted to.

But if he stuck with his "no" answer, would he lose her? Could this be an all-or-nothing deal with her?

Sure, Zach had always been like a brother to him. Eric had never trusted anyone more in his life. And he knew if anybody could make this work, it would be the three of them.

But *shit*…

She laid an easy hand on his chest, spread her fingers and dug into his pecs. He soaked her warmth into his heart.

"Please don't be angry with Zach over this, Eric. We both want you to understand the depth of what you mean to us. All we want is to share our love, to share the love we all have for each other…"

A small part of his rage eased away as his body tightened further against her touch. Mentally? Yeah, he got it. Could appreciate her rationale. But in his heart… *Damn it.*

"Lil." Her name burned his throat as he lifted his gaze to Zach. "I've never been as close to any man as I am to you. I'd lay my life down, anytime, anyplace, if it meant you'd both be safe. But this..."

"I know." Zach loosened his arms and lowered his hands into the pockets of his jeans, then sidestepped to stand directly behind Lily. When his chest touched her shoulder, her eyes drifted shut and she held her breath. He closed in and tenderly kissed the side of her neck. A delicate moan fell from her lips. The eroticism of the simple gesture pushed Eric closer to that narrow edge of control.

"You love her," Zach lifted his head and stared into his eyes. "And so do I." He withdrew his hands from his pockets, brought them under her arms, and then spanned them over her stomach. Eric thought he'd die when Zach's thumbs teased the underside of the black lacy bra. "All we're asking for here is a chance to see where this goes. A chance to find something beyond the typical 'everyday' kind of love. A chance for...well, *more*."

Eric squeezed his eyes shut. Oh Jesus, he wanted *more*, too. After a year and a half of barely living, existing only to survive, the crushing realization of wanting what they offered hit with the force of a fully loaded Blackhawk helicopter. Right then, he knew he couldn't live without her—or Zach either for that matter.

He opened his eyes. The desire and need etched upon both their faces... *Now* he understood. He brushed his hands across Zach's as the other man caressed Lily's stomach. Their gazes caught before Eric lowered his hands to grasp her hips. "Come here, Lil."

She sucked in another breath and slid into his arms. He gathered her close and held tight.

"I want you so much, babe. But this...this is so damn hard for me. To share you... God, with anyone..."

"Eric..."

He skimmed her lower back with his rough, calloused hands. Fuck, her skin felt so amazing under his touch. His cock swelled to amazing lengths just from her heat, her softness. And he couldn't help it, he had to taste her. He lowered his mouth and nipped along her shoulder. The hiss she released as his teeth grazed over her sensitive skin speared him.

She blazed within his arms and he instantly drew up an image in his mind of her nestled the way she was now between him and Zach. But tighter, and writhing as they made love to her slowly, torturously. She'd be sweet, so supple and more gorgeous than ever before.

Damn it to hell. He didn't know if he loved or hated how that little vision sealed the deal.

He had to do this. Wanted to do this more than anything. For her. Oh Christ, for all of them.

He tangled his hand in her hair and pulled her head back, then kissed her with everything he had in him. On a groan, she lifted to her toes and returned his passion with a sultry desperation that matched his own. She reached back at the same time, found Zach's hand and pulled him closer.

Fire. God, she was on fucking fire. The fingers of her free hand fisted the collar of his shirt. Her hips ground against his as Zach closed in behind her and once again wrapped an arm around her. Sure he'd lose control any second, Eric broke from their kiss, spun her away from Zach and slid an arm under her knees. Her head fell against his shoulder when he lifted her into his arms. After a step toward the hallway, and with Lily's hand still holding onto Zach's, he plastered his best friend with a heated stare over his opposite shoulder.

"Bedroom. Now. You coming?"

Zach's blood shot through his veins as his heart rate picked up double-time. "Hell yeah. Couldn't keep me away."

He still gripped Lily's hand as they made their way down the hallway to the bedroom. Once there, he let go and flicked on the small crystal lamp on her dresser. The mellow glow bathed the room with just enough light to see by.

Eric laid her on the bed, slid his body over hers while Zach pulled the shirt over his head. His muscles bunched in anticipation, his cock hardened to steel. The radiance on Lily's face wrecked the tentative hold Zach had on his control. He wanted this so badly, but he also needed to pull back on that desire some or he'd lose it. No way did he want this to be over too quickly.

She held out her hand. "Come lie with us, Zach. Right here, next to me."

Heat rushed him when he enveloped her dainty fingers in his grip, climbed onto the bed and settled next to them.

Man, this felt so fucking right.

Her eyes glistened with happy tears. Zach leaned closer to kiss away a drop that hung on the edge of her lashes. Her chin quivered when she smiled and a little more of his control slipped further away. He wanted her, ached for her so damn much.

She tilted her head and kissed him with a tenderness he hadn't yet experienced with her. Their one night together had been so urgent, so frantic. But he loved this side of her, too.

Eric nuzzled her neck as Zach sucked the tip of Lily's tongue into his mouth. The inferno in his friend's eyes was unmistakable when he moved to lick along her ear and their gazes caught again.

Zach groaned and broke away. Lily cupped Eric's cheek then, angled her lips to meet with his for a quick, scorching kiss.

"You're the world to me, baby." Eric soothed her with gentle nudges from his lips, tender caresses on her cheeks with his thumbs. "If this is truly what you want, I'm in. All the way. All I want is for you…for *us* to be happy."

She drew her hand over Eric's stubbled head, and then turned back to Zach. He entwined his fingers with hers and nibbled on the inside of her wrist.

"That's all any of us wants," Zach added. "The most we could ever hope for."

With an easy thumb on her chin, Eric leaned in and rekindled his kiss. Their breaths rasped together, their tongues dueled. Zach thought his cock would explode from the sight.

Eric pulled back. Desire, along with love—the heart-wrenching, be-all, end-all kind of love—spilled from Lily's gaze. She then struck Zach just as hard with the exact same adoration and passion.

Paradise itself couldn't be this perfect.

"You ready for this, sugar?" Zach pressed his lips to the back of her hand, grazed the edge of her bra with an inquisitive finger. "Ready to take all of us to that next level?"

The tip of her wet, pink tongue glossed her bottom lip. Her hips circled under Eric.

"Oh God, yes. More than either of you could know."

Yeah, Zach seriously doubted that. He had a fairly good idea of how ready she really was.

Of how ready they all were.

Chapter Seven

Lily's body hummed while her heart soared. She knew she'd start sobbing from their heartfelt words if Eric hadn't slid to his side and gathered her in his arms. The pressure of him at her front and Zach against her back lifted her to new heights. The hot kisses they trailed on either side of her neck thrilled her beyond reason.

After everything that happened earlier, she couldn't believe she now lay between the two men she loved more than anything. Their searing heat, along with their solid walls of muscles, surrounded her. The overwhelming love coming from each of them made that Texas-sized knot in her throat return, but for an entirely different reason this time.

She wasn't so sure she hadn't died and gone to heaven.

But when Zach skimmed her bra strap down her shoulder and scraped his teeth along the tender skin there, she knew this was more than real. The undeniable certainty of what they were about to do heated her from the inside out.

Eric possessed her mouth again, consumed her in another devastating kiss. When he ran his tongue over hers, the smoky flavor of the whiskey from earlier tingled along her taste buds. She cradled his head in one hand to bring him closer as the other wrapped around Zach's at her shoulder. A low moan escaped her throat at the combination of nonstop sensations.

She tangled her fingers in Zach's hair and gave a tug. When he chuckled, the vibration danced along the skin on her back. "Naughty, naughty, love. I'll have to get you back for that."

Eric broke free of her mouth, only to move lower to her chin and neck. The wicked little bites he bombarded her with had her sex clenching in need.

"Can't wait," she replied, more than a bit breathless.

She felt Zach's grin on her shoulder. "I'll just bet you can't."

He shifted and moved her so she lay on her back. Eric never stopped his torturous kisses, only now he worked his way past her collarbone to the rise of her breast. Zach snaked his hand under her and with an expert flick of his fingers, unclasped her bra. With coordinated moves, each man pulled a strap off her arm until she was bared to their stares. Then their mouths—oh, their sinful mouths—covered her, right where she needed them most. Rough tongues flicked both nipples, sharp teeth bit before heated lips covered the sting.

They sucked. They licked. They drove her completely mad.

One unbuttoned her jeans. The other lowered the zipper. Together they drew the pants over her hips and down her thighs. Zach left her breast, kissed along her quivering stomach until he came to the edge of the lace thong she wore. He pushed her jeans the rest of the way off, let them fall to the floor and continued the sweet torture of his mouth.

She could barely hold a complete thought, her mind whirled. But one thing she knew for certain, she wanted to touch them. Needed to touch them. She yanked at Eric's camouflage shirt, pulled it and the beige t-shirt underneath off together in one swift motion.

Eric pushed himself to his knees. His hands went to his belt buckle and Lily swallowed. Zach was wreaking havoc on the inside of her thighs with his sinful mouth, but she couldn't help but stare at Eric as he unbuckled, unbuttoned and slowly—God, too slowly—drew his own zipper down.

"Eighteen months without you, Lil. A fucking year and a half." He slid backward off the bed. His feet hit the floor and he stood at the edge. "The one thing I fantasized about most on those long nights alone? Your mouth. On me."

Lily groaned and grabbed her breast with one hand, pinched her nipple until a sweet, erotic pain shot through her while the other clenched again between her legs, twisted in Zach's hair.

Eric peeled his Marine-issued camos open and pushed them past a pair of plain boxer briefs. The low-rise waistband showed off the sexy cut of his sculpted abs, the front panel not standing a chance at concealing the impressive erection hidden behind it.

Zach picked that moment to kiss her through the lace of her panties. She sucked in a quick breath, ground against his mouth, but never broke eye contact with Eric. Her heart beat so fast. Her mouth watered at what she knew Eric wanted, at what Zach was already doing.

Eric stepped out of his pants and stuffed his hand inside his boxers. He gripped himself, stroked slow and licked his lips.

God, she wanted to be the one doing that to him. "Don't tease me, Eric. I can't take it. Please..." The words no sooner left her lips when Zach pushed aside her thong and dipped his tongue inside her. Her hips bucked off the bed. "Ah...*yes*..."

Her breath got stuck somewhere in her lungs as Zach drew his tongue through her sex to settle on her clit. Her head spun, her blood raced. She fisted Zach's hair tighter and leaned up on one elbow. Breathy, she said to Eric, "Come here, baby. Let's make this reality kick ass against all those fantasies."

He smiled and she got a thrill at knowing she lightened his heart some. He shucked his boxers and knelt next to her on the bed.

He was so beautiful. Tight, tanned skin covered hard, warrior muscles.

Her soldier, her hero.

With a hand holding the base of his shaft, his other shakily caressed her cheek. She inched forward and circled the head of his cock with her tongue before taking him fully in her mouth. He groaned and lifted his face to the ceiling. She stilled for a moment and then withdrew to suck gently on the tip. On a hiss between clenched teeth, he lowered his head and blasted her with a stare that all but screamed his hot, heavy desire. When he threaded his fingers through her hair to hold her nape, she eased even more, let him take full control.

He fucked her mouth, slow and easy as Zach's in turn shattered every dream she'd held about this moment. It was more, oh so much more than she ever imagined. Zach danced his tongue over her clit as she moaned around Eric's engorged cock.

Close, yes…yes…so close.

"That's it, Lily-sweet," Eric panted on a quicker thrust. "Let's do this together. You ready to come with me? It's been so damn long. Too damn long. I can't last…"

As he said the words, Zach shifted, pulled her thong off, then returned his mouth to her and thrust a finger hard inside her. Fire raced up her spine, tremors shook her thighs. She relaxed her throat as every other muscle in her body tightened, and took Eric even deeper.

"Ahh…yes… Just like that, sweetheart." Another firm lunge in her mouth. Another low groan. Eric clenched his jaw and fisted her hair, pulled it. She had always reveled in his rawness, his stark masculinity. But this…this rough but contrastingly tender way he was taking her… God, she loved it.

"Now, baby. Christ, *now*."

The pulsations from Eric's cock as he slid down her throat and the provocative sting from the grip he had on her hair, mixed with Zach's expert touches, sent her flying over the edge. She bucked against Zach's mouth in an attempt to deepen his fingers as she swallowed every bit of Eric's release.

He shouted her name, an anguished cry of desperation and need as he stilled inside her mouth. Lily came with a charge as fierce as any lightening bolt. Pleasure slammed into every cell of her body while Zach continued to wring out the jolts her climax created.

Eric slipped from her mouth and flopped back on the bed. Zach crawled up her body with tiny kisses and nips. Still breathing hard, she mewled when Zach placed his lips over hers. The taste of herself on his tongue renewed the tingle in her belly and she suddenly realized he'd shed his pants at some point. He covered her sweat-damp body, his heated skin adhering to hers, his hard cock like a steel rod against her thigh.

"That was so fucking hot, babe," he whispered, then licked along her earlobe. "But I think you killed the poor guy."

She giggled, light and free, and glanced at Eric. He lay next to them with one arm over his eyes, his chest rising and falling in short breaths. When the edge of his lip quirked, his devilish dimple gleamed at her.

"Damn near. To think I lived through mortar attacks only to be taken out by a blow job." He lifted his arm and looked at them. "A perfect blow job, I have to add."

Zach nuzzled under her ear. "Perfect, huh?" He licked down the hollow of her neck, then nibbled over her shoulder as his hands stroked along her sides. "I'd love to feel some of that perfection, too, babe. Like now."

"Now, hmm?" she teased.

"Oh, yeah. I'm dying here."

"Well, never let it be said I wouldn't accommodate a dying man." She shoved at his shoulders until he rolled onto his back. Straddling his narrow hips, she caressed his rough jaw and leaned down for a quick kiss before creating a trail of nips and licks over his chest. She paid special attention to his peaked nipples, and then went lower to scrape her teeth along his ribs. The muscles of his six-pack tightened as she brushed her tongue across the hard ridges. She grasped his swollen shaft in her right hand, stroked it once as she lowered further to enclose the near-purple head in her mouth. Zach's hips lifted and his hand pushed on the crown of her head.

"Fuck, *yes*..."

She grinned to herself as she took as much of his length as she could. The width stretched her lips just as Eric's had, the thick vein along the underside pulsed against her tongue. She reached down, grabbed his sac and pulled gently.

"Oh hell, Lil," he groaned. He thrust upward in time with her down strokes, and glanced to Eric. "Yeah, man. Perfect. Absolutely perfect."

The bed shifted when Eric moved closer. While on her hands and knees over Zach's legs, Eric twisted until his face came even with her ass, his knees next to Zach's trim waist.

"Looks pretty damn perfect from back here, too," he said. Warm lips nudged her left cheek, a hot hand rose between her thighs.

Zach lifted his head at the same time Eric brushed his fingers over the short, trimmed hairs of her mound. Easing higher, he slipped a finger inside her. She tightened around it and groaned.

While lifting his free hand behind his head, Zach drew her into his stare. Eyes hooded, the deep brown shade of his irises had darkened to nearly coal black. His bicep bulged beside his temple, his pecs flexed over his chest with power and strength.

"What's he doing there, babe? Are his fingers inside your sweet body? God, I know he can feel how tight you are, how wet."

At his words, Eric thrust again, the first finger joined by another, his mouth moving closer to her core.

She arched her back and tingles spread throughout her womb. With a moan she took Zach faster, and her world began to spin off its axis. A muscle jumped in his jaw when she slowed to scrape her teeth gently upward, ending with little bites on the velvet-soft tip, only to delve deeper once more.

"That's good, baby. So damn good..." He thrust harder, somehow in time with Eric's fingers as he buried them inside her, retreated, and then plunged all over again. She couldn't stand it, she needed to come again. Desperately.

She snuck her hand through her legs, under Eric's, to find the hard nub of her over-sensitive clit. Eric had her juices flowing from the attention of his skilled fingers, she was completely soaked. She stroked herself once, twice. All the while, Zach watched her with an expression of passion and love.

"Oh yeah, Lil. Touch yourself... I want you to come with me, too." All she could manage in answer was a strangled moan. "Do this for me, sweetheart. Oh God... Come with me..."

At that moment, Eric twisted his hand. Her sex clenched as he stroked her G-spot over and over while she rubbed furiously on her clit. But when he leaned closer to her ass, pressed a kiss on her lower back, then drew his tongue lower...and then lower still...down the crevice until his hot tongue rimmed the tender skin around her anus...

Oh God...

She groaned with a jagged cry around Zach's cock.

The unexpected erotic sensation, so different from anything she'd ever experienced before, sent her spinning off into sheer oblivion. When her body shook, then tensed in a fierce orgasm, she squeezed her eyes shut, locked her jaw and sucked on Zach harder. She opened her eyes a moment later, uneven breaths rasping through her nose as Zach's abs and legs tightened under her. He caught her gaze and growled—a guttural, almost carnal sound—before bringing the hand from behind his head. He grabbed onto Eric's thigh at his side in a brutal grip. His hips bucked, his cock jerked inside her mouth. Spurts of his salty release shot down her throat, and she greedily swallowed all she could.

She shuddered with her own sweet tremors as Eric slowed the pace of his fingers and nuzzled her rear with a scratchy cheek. She gave Zach's cock one final lick, and then dropped to her side between the two hard men. Zach released Eric's thigh, wrapped that arm tight around her waist and squeezed. Eric spun to snuggle up behind her, all the while raining kisses along her upper arm.

"Somebody said something before about dying?" she gasped.

Both men chuckled, but Zach spoke first. "Oh, no, sweetness. We're not letting you off that easy."

She playfully bit his shoulder. "Not what I meant. I just feel… This is heaven for me."

Eric whispered in her ear as he stroked her hip. "Let us take you higher…"

She shivered at his simple words, at his erotic touches.

"Stratosphere awaits, babe," Zach added, his lips gentle on her forehead, his still-raspy breaths warm across her skin.

They rolled her within their arms so she faced Eric and Zach lay behind her. He pressed his mouth to her shoulder, got up from the bed and picked up his pants. As he dug in the pocket and pulled out a couple condoms, he headed to her nightstand and opened the drawer. He smiled at her then, a bottle of lubricant in hand.

"As I suspected," he said on a chuckle. "Every woman's hiding place."

She squirmed a bit within Eric's grasp, knowing exactly why Zach would need the lube.

Eric whispered in her ear. "We'll take it slow, just to make sure you're ready. The last thing either of us wants is to hurt you."

She licked her lips as Zach tossed his pants aside and crawled back on the bed.

"I know," she answered. "But I'm so ready. I've waited for this, for both of you, for so long."

Eric kissed her, slow and sensual. With a lick to her bottom lip, he said, "Lie on top of me, Lil. Take me inside you."

Her belly fluttered along with her heart at the words. He held her tight, rocked them until he lay on his back. With her legs arranged at his sides, he pushed on her shoulders for her to sit upright. His cock, hard and long once again, rubbed against her clit as she sat astride him.

"Go ahead," he said, eyes blazing into hers, hands stroking her thighs. "Take me in your hand. Put me inside you."

Zach came up behind her. His knees straddled Eric's legs, his hands gripped her hips. He licked up her neck and brushed his chest against her back, his cock against her rear. When she paused for a split second, Zach took her hand in his and brought it between her legs. Together they rolled a condom on Eric, and then wrapped their fingers around his sheathed cock. She lifted up and they placed him at the entrance to her body. Zach pushed down on her hip with his free hand and all three groaned in unison as she impaled herself on Eric.

"I love you," Zach whispered in her ear. She lifted her arm behind her head, cupped his nape and turned into his kiss. She stayed like that for several moments, moving leisurely to adjust her body to Eric's width, kissing Zach slow and easy. Loving every second of it.

Breathless, Zach broke the kiss. "Don't get too far ahead of me, babe." He pulled her hand from his neck and gently eased her down until she lay on Eric's chest. The light hairs on his hard pecs brushed along her nipples. Tingles soared through her breasts at the ticklish sensation.

Eric took his turn at her mouth with a kiss so hot her toes curled. He lifted his hips, drove harder inside her. But when

Zach's finger, coated with the cool, thick jelly, delved down the crevice of her ass, she nearly came undone.

He circled her anus, lubricating her gently, and then slid the tip of one finger past the tight ring of muscles. At first reaction, her body wanted to refuse him. He caressed her ass cheek, soothed her with a quiet, "Easy now…"

After another quick thrust, Eric held her hips still. Every muscle in her body screamed to move against them.

"Hold on a sec, Lil. Let him do this. We don't want to hurt you. Just relax and feel."

She held his gaze, so full of love her heart ached, and breathed through Zach deepening his finger.

"That's my girl. You can do this, Lil. Breathe again…"

She moaned as Zach added another finger, her body accepting him more easily now. Eric closed his eyes and swallowed. She passed her lips gently over his. "You feel him, too. Don't you?"

He nodded and opened his eyes. "Yeah, babe. I do."

She bit her lower lip and squeezed her eyes as another rush of cold lubricant accompanied yet another finger. She burned inside, the slight pain a heady contrast to the overwhelming pleasure of Zach's fingers.

Eric held her cheek in his palm. "Open your eyes, sweetheart. Tell me what you feel."

She couldn't. It was too much, she felt too much. The fullness of Eric, the bite from Zach. She reared back with a sudden urgent need to move against them both.

*More…*she had to have more…

Zach held her down with a hot hand between her shoulder blades. "Lil. Give me another second…"

"No! Now, Zach. God, please, now…"

"Take her…" Eric added with a growl through clenched teeth.

She glanced over her shoulder, breathless and on the verge of tears. Zach ripped the condom wrapper open with his teeth, sheathed himself in a heartbeat. He coated himself with the lubricant and edged forward.

She laid her head on Eric's shoulder as Zach prodded her rear entrance. "Push against me. Easy..."

Following his instructions, she opened herself to him. When the head of his cock slipped in, she grabbed Eric's biceps in a death hold. Zach retreated, thrust again. She bit Eric's shoulder as both men groaned.

Zach wrapped a hand over her shoulder. His strong fingers dug into the muscles at the side of her neck. "God, you're so fucking tight." Another few inches eased inside her. "Holy hell, love."

Eric moved then, and she nearly fell apart. The dual sensations were more than she could've ever prepared for. The heat from their bodies and the love pouring from each of them only added to the rush of the moment.

This was what she wanted.

As the men found their rhythm, she knew she could never go back to the way things were before. Eric and Zach—together—were her future. Her home. Her life.

"You okay?" Eric asked.

Cocooned between the two men she loved? How could she not be okay? "Oh, Eric, it's so much more..."

She braced her hands on his chest, lifted up and thrust back. Every nerve ending blazed, every cell inside her shattered.

"You're so beautiful like this, Lil..." Eric stroked her breasts, and then pinched her nipples as Zach kissed her shoulder. Their speed increased, their bodies glistened with a fine sheen of sweat.

Lily's head spun. She tightened on them both. When she moaned and tossed her head back, Eric followed suit. He left her breasts, reached behind her and grabbed onto Zach.

Holding his ass, Eric pulled him hard. The action pushed Zach further into her and her clit rubbed over the base of Eric's cock.

Again and again…over and over. She was coming apart, drowning in a pool of raw power and heated flesh. Her legs began to tremble as the familiar tingle of her orgasm took root.

Eric groaned. "She's coming… Ah fuck, I can feel her coming…"

"Let loose, babe," Zach said. We're with you…right here with you."

Her entire body lit in a carnal explosion. Every sensation enhanced with a gleaming clarity. She felt them come inside her, the jolt from Eric, the pulsation of Zach behind her.

She never imagined it would be like this.

"God, I love you, Lil." Eric's voice was low, raw, as Zach breathed his own words into her ear.

"Love you so much, Lily."

Through the moans, the fierce grips and the heat of wandering lips, Lily's love grew to a level she'd only dreamed of. These were her men. They belonged to her and her to them. Nothing would change that.

Nothing ever could.

They collapsed into a heap of sticky skin and tangled limbs. Her muscles turned to liquid, her mind to mush. Zach left from behind her and padded to the bathroom. He returned with a warm towel, cleaned her quickly before tossing the cloth into her hamper and snuggling under the covers with her and Eric.

Eric stifled a yawn and Lily chuckled. "Tired?"

Her front to his, he tucked her head under his chin as Zach settled in behind her. "It's been a long day, and you two just kicked my ass, big time." He stroked his thumb over her hip. "I've got to wonder, though, is this what we can always expect?"

She smiled and little tingles danced under his touch. "I hope so. All I know is I'm never happier than when I'm with the two of you. I love both of you so much for trusting in me, for trusting in the love I have for each of you."

She shifted a little to look at Zach over her shoulder. "I love you, Zach. You've been my rock these last few months. That means more to me than I could ever put into words."

"Ah, Lil, you know I love you." He quirked his lip. "Something in me always has. I'm addicted to everything about you."

The comment had her glowing from the inside out. She then cupped Eric's cheek.

"I love you so much, Eric. My heart's complete now that you're back home, safe and sound."

"Lily, babe. It's always been you. I've been in love with you forever."

If possible, she lit up inside even more. "I want this to work more than anything. I know in my heart we can make a life together, just like this."

Zach spoke up then. "As long as we're honest and never hold back what we're feeling, we can. I'm talking forever here, guys. You two are everything to me. My love, my family."

Her heart melted. "Family. I love the sound of that."

Eric brushed the hair from her shoulder. "Me too, Lil. Me too. You've won your war. We're here, and we're all yours."

UNSCRIPTED

Dedication

To my late sister, who proved to me that every soul possesses the ability to heal, regardless of less than favorable and oftentimes challenging circumstances. I miss her, every single day.

And to Jen and Heather – your support and wisdom push me to be the absolute best I can be, and I thank you both for your unending encouragement.

Trademarks Acknowledgement

The author acknowledges the trademarked status and trademark owners of the following wordmarks mentioned in this work of fiction:

Ray-Ban: Luxottica S.r.l.

Variety: Variety, Inc.

Chapter One

Pink.

A too-fucking-tight pink t-shirt.

The bright color matched the nail polish on Brynn Lang's dainty fingernails and on her more-than-suckable bubble-gum toes. Toes that drove Ryan Manning crazy when she wriggled them against the beach towel spread out underneath her on the chaise lounge.

But God, the t-shirt. Stretched the way it was, the thin cotton left nothing to the imagination. Then again, Ryan really didn't need his imagination. He knew that body, and knew it well. The scent of her. The taste of her. Every unforgettable sound she ever made while he was inside her. He knew it all too well.

It felt like forever since he last touched her. His palms itched to run them over her silky skin and he had to fist his hands at his sides to fight back the urge. His body may not care how different things were now, but his mind sure as hell wouldn't let him forget that every single bit of that difference was his own fault.

And it was way past time for him to atone for all he'd done.

Even though they'd figured it a long shot, Ryan and his talent agent had negotiated for two weeks straight to get the starring role in what was considered to be Hollywood's next big blockbuster film offered to him after a horrific car accident sidelined the first actor hired. But Ryan would've scribbled his John Hancock on the contract without ever looking at it—so long as Brynn was still signed on to be the co-star.

He knew she'd despise seeing him again, and honestly he couldn't blame her. Their relationship—if you could even put that sort of label on the three-month-long blazing affair they'd had—had ended on the opposite side of the ideal spectrum. Again, not that there was anyone to blame for that but himself. At the end, he'd been more than a prick to her and hurt her badly enough that her silent damnation that final night would ring in his ears louder than any words she could've screamed at him.

God, how he'd messed things up.

Fate, to him, had always been a cold, fickle bitch. But for the first time in years things were finally going his way. He'd worked hard—damn hard—to turn his life and reputation around, but there was still a lot he'd done in his past he needed to make up for. Second chances like this one were few and far between. No way in hell would he fuck it up this go-round.

The number one item on his to-do list was to make amends with Brynn. Coming in a very close second was for him to do what he should've done in the first damn place.

Make her his for good.

He stood just inside the veranda doorway of the resort as she lounged poolside and flipped through the pages of *Variety* magazine. The waitstaff doted on her, but she never asked for much. Would she like a refill on her iced tea? Sure, that'd be great. An extra towel? No, not right now, thank you.

The small yet classy haven the production company had taken over had that picture-perfect quality about it. Nestled between rolling hills and an often rocky coastline, the location wasn't too far from the private studio where they'd begin shooting tomorrow. Everyone around him was geared up to get started on the movie, and at times like these tensions usually ran high. Hell, he was nearly on overload himself.

But not Brynn. She was so calm. Cool.

Together.

He'd been lurking in the shadows of the lobby when she checked in a few hours ago and had to all but stuff his tongue back in his mouth at the drop-dead sexy way her body swayed when she walked to the elevator to head to her room. And he'd still been sitting in the same place when she came back down an hour later wearing that damn pink t-shirt and the matching skimpy bottoms to go to the pool.

She hadn't really changed much from the last time he'd seen her, which was, man, a little over six months ago. At least he didn't think she'd changed. So much about that last night with her was pretty fuzzy.

He squeezed his eyes shut and drew in a calming breath. *Fuck,* fuzzy nothing. By the time the shit hit the fan that night, he'd been way more than three sheets to the wind. But even at that, he still remembered the most agonizing parts.

"Someone's going to accuse you of stalking, you know."

He turned to find Reggie, his studio-assigned assistant, sauntering up beside him. Ryan lifted the edge of his lip in a half-smile and returned his gaze to Brynn just in time to see her wrap her lips around the straw in her drink. Christ, the sight of her puckering up like that… His entire body stiffened just thinking about how her lips used to wrap around *him* like that. The memories made him rock-hard in an instant.

"Possibly. They wouldn't be too far off, either."

"Well, I can't say as I blame you. She's gorgeous."

Ryan dipped his Ray-Bans to the end of his nose, crossed his arms over his chest and pierced the other man with a vicious stare while a low, primal growl rose from his chest. He never really was one for all that testosterone-laced alpha-male grunting and posturing, but this time he couldn't help it. Reggie would only get this one warning to stay away from Brynn. Far, far away from her.

The young man took a step back and held up his hands in submission. "Completely out of my league, though. No worries there, Mr. Manning."

Ryan relaxed barely a fraction. Okay, so he didn't have a firm link to Brynn anymore, no real right to warn the kid off, but the need to stake his claim where she was concerned rode him hard. Ever since leaving rehab three months ago, he'd been waiting for the perfect opportunity to get closer to her, to find the perfect way to apologize.

Then out of the blue, word trickled down about how the studio needed to fill this part along with who the co-star was. That's when Ryan decided that maybe Ms. Cold-Hearted-Fate wasn't such a capricious bitch after all.

Reggie cleared his throat as Ryan turned his attention back to Brynn. "The schedule for tomorrow was just released. You're to report to the set at seven."

"What's the scene?" he asked casually, never taking his eyes off her. Everything about Brynn Lang enraptured him and he found he couldn't tear himself away even though he ought to use this downtime to go over the script again. The other members of the cast had had theirs for a while now, but he wouldn't let that discourage him. He exuded professionalism nowadays and had taken every opportunity to study the screenplay since he signed the contract. Good thing, too. Since movies were never shot in sequential order, he needed to be ready for whatever the higher-ups threw at him. More than likely they'd be on a soundstage for the next few days shooting the interior scenes, with the outdoor action scenes to follow sometime later.

Reggie flipped through papers and schedules and God knew whatever else the kid had attached to the clipboard in his hands. But when Reg lifted his gaze and met Ryan's with a smirky grin, he knew exactly which scene it was.

Reggie's grin widened as he waggled his eyebrows. "It's your lucky day, Mr. Manning. It just so happens to be the final love scene between you and Ms. Lang."

Well, hell. Didn't that little bit of info instantly make Ryan fall head-over-heels in love with the now perfect Ms. Fate.

*****

God, it felt so good to be on a movie set again.

Her head heavy from the weight of huge hot rollers, Brynn Lang sat in front of the brightly lit mirror in the makeup trailer waiting for her artist, Roman, to finish with the final touch-up of her lip gloss before he moved on to style her hair. And since the first scene they were working on this morning was the end love scene, this visit to her old friend would be her only stop. A trip to the costume trailer wouldn't be necessary.

Yee haw.

"Any word on who they replaced Trevor with?"

Brynn shook her head as a tingle of nerves rattled through her insides. "When I got the call yesterday morning, I didn't even think to ask. I was just so thrilled they found somebody." She fiddled with the sash on her robe, winding and unwinding the tie around her index finger. A nervous gesture, she supposed, but repeating the action was better than some of the alternative inane diversions she could think of.

"You know, it might've been a mistake, but I agreed to forgo the rehearsals for the first few days along with whatever else the production assistant asked. Frankly, I barely heard a word he said past *We found someone and need to get a move on this.* The *right now* he tossed in at the end made me a little nervous, too. I hung up the phone, packed right up and hopped on the first flight back."

"Honey, the least they could've done was tell you who you were going to get naked with. That they didn't is just *so* cruel." Roman gave her a quick teasing wink in the mirror as he started to pull the rollers from her hair.

She smiled back and huffed out a breath. "Honestly, I don't care who it is. I'm just grateful they signed someone. I've been on pins and needles wondering if the movie was even going to happen at all."

"You, me and the rest of the crew, darlin'."

"Leave it to sweet Trevor to pull one of his stunts and flip his car, what was it? Five times? He knew how much I was relying on this job, Roman."

Brynn was counting on this film to boost her stagnant career. Starring in one too many high-school pictures in her early twenties had given her the unwelcome status of being Hollywood's one-time favorite teen-queen. Now, at twenty-nine, she needed this hard-driving, big budget flick in order to change her reputation from a has-been teen idol into a serious and respected actress. And that Trevor McNight came this close to screwing that up irritated her beyond belief.

"I'm just thankful the producers decided to go ahead with filming after his accident. They could've just as easily shut down the set and cashed in on the production insurance."

What would she have done then?

"Amen to that, hon. I need this job, too." After a final quick spray, Roman grinned from behind her and leaned down next to her ear. When their eyes met in the mirror, his were full of compassion and pride. "Relax, okay? I just know you're gonna knock 'em dead today. And whoever they found to replace Trevor better be thanking his lucky stars. It's not every day a man gets to make love to someone as gorgeous and sexy as you, even if it isn't for real."

She cupped his jaw and planted a kiss on his smooth cheek. "Thank you, Roman. You really are the best."

He fanned himself with a dramatic flutter of his eyelashes. "You and I both know that, honey, but someone needs to inform Chace Crawford of that delicious little fact. Or Cindy Crawford. Hell I'd take either one. I'm not picky."

She waggled her finger and laughed. "You know, I take back everything nice I ever said about you. You're horrible."

With a spin of her chair, he laughed too and held his hand out in a gallant gesture. "Off you go, my lovely. I'll see you on set in a bit for the final touch-ups."

After another quick kiss on his cheek, she pounced through the door of the trailer and out into the early morning, southern California sunshine. A quick tug on the belt of her robe, and she hopped down the stairs and headed toward the soundstage, her thin pink slippers soundless against the hard pavement. Despite the morning's mild temperature, she shivered a little as a gentle breeze flitted under the hem of the robe. She rationalized the goose bumps by chalking it up to being completely naked under the satin, except of course for the sticky little modesty patch she'd put on earlier, and told herself the reaction had nothing to do with the nerves skittering around inside her. Every actor was a little apprehensive before filming the first scene of a major movie. Right?

But, boy oh boy, this wasn't just any first scene.

She grabbed hold of the door handle and clutched the edges of the robe at her knees. She held on to both for dear life as an uneasy panic weaved its way through her gut. Heaven above, the stark reality of what she was about to do just hit her.

A love scene. An *I'm nude, you're nude, we're both sweaty and* nude *in front of forty strangers* love scene.

Yes, she'd read the script over and over, knew this was *the* pivotal moment in the movie for the lead characters' relationship. She'd even gone so far as to have an in-depth conversation with Trevor about how they were going to handle the whole scenario once the time came. He really was a sweet guy, despite his twisted passion for adrenaline. And being more experienced, he'd been able to put her mind at ease by telling her repeatedly that sex scenes, regardless of how steamy and provocative they appeared onscreen, didn't come anywhere close to being so while filming them.

And didn't it just figure that now he was off at some fancy-schmancy rehabilitation center in the mountains with, knowing him, a bevy of gorgeous physical therapists rubbing out this kink or that muscle cramp while she was getting ready to pretend to do the nasty without him.

What she'd really love to do right now was wring his ever-loving neck.

But as much as the trepidation stopped her cold in her tracks, she *had* to go through with this. Backing out now was *not* an option. This picture was her big chance, the light at the end of her tunnel. If she couldn't go on, if she froze up…

No, she wouldn't. Her career depended on keeping a cool head. This was business. Her profession. Nothing more.

Pushing all the tingles and butterflies away, she twisted the knob, drew in a breath and stepped over the threshold into the dark soundstage. In the southeast corner was the set of her character's apartment where the scene would be filmed. She headed over with her head held high and confidence in her stride.

Never let 'em see you sweat. Yep, that old adage was her new motto.

And now she had to stick to it.

The on-set production assistant gave her a fake, practiced smile and rattled off a ten-second rundown of the morning's schedule. "You're the first on set. We're just waiting for Mr. Manning, then we can get started."

As her head snapped around to glare at him, the skinny, semi-nerdy guy actually took a quick step back.

"Mr. *who*?" She asked the question calmly enough, even though alarms started blaring inside her head.

"Um, Manning. Ryan Manning. Didn't they tell you?"

A bubble of anger rose from her stomach and burst into an aching fizz inside her chest at the same time a familiar, yet unwelcome, erotic tingle seared between her legs. Never in a million years would she have considered that Ryan would be the actor they'd found to replace Trevor. Hell, she was surprised the jackass was still alive at all. She figured by now he'd either be six feet under, or washed up in some two-bit town asking the next customer in line, "Would you like fries with that?"

Ha, maybe it was a good thing he *was* still alive. Because even though at one time she wanted nothing more than to spend all day tangled in bed with him, right now she'd love nothing more than having the chance to kill him herself.

"No," she answered, forcing a calm to her demeanor she certainly didn't feel. "They didn't."

"Oh, well. Yeah," the kid stammered. "He should be here any minute." He cocked his head slightly and studied her with a brief expression of sincerity. "Everything okay?"

Giving in to the sudden wave of panic by hiding in a corner somewhere or causing an uproar by shooting this scrawny little PA-turned-messenger wouldn't help the situation any, although everything inside her screamed to pick one or the other and go for it with all her gusto. But rather than that, she pasted on a half-smile, casually tossed her hair over her shoulder and lied her Pilates-toned ass off. "Fine. Everything's just fine."

The PA checked his watch with a returning detached indifference. "Good," he said to her, and then spoke to the crew through the mic in his headset. "Okay, people, half the talent is here—" When a noisy commotion behind the cameras stole his attention, he stalked off, muttering as he went about competence and how the lack thereof would surely knock them off schedule, and wasn't that just a great way to lead off the filming schedule. He left Brynn alone to deal with the personal turmoil his laid-back disclosure had caused.

Ryan Manning? God, how could she be so unlucky? Yes, she'd tried her damndest to not dwell on what he'd done—well, not too much anyway—and had even fooled herself enough to believe that she'd come to terms with all the hurt. She truly thought she'd let her hatred for him go.

But at times like this when his name was bantered about, or when she'd glimpse an old picture of him looking all suave and beyond-reasonable sexy, all the once-forgotten anger—along with that crazy, insatiable desire—would come back in a swift rush.

Yes, he'd embarrassed her. And played on her emotions. But more than any of that, he'd hurt her to the core.

"Brynn?"

Her spine stiffened at the deep voice behind her. The unforgettable tone dripped with sensuality and the mellow pitch seeped over her senses like a thick cosmic goo determined to suffocate her.

Ryan.

She closed her eyes and gripped the knot on her robe's sash tighter. Okay, she could do this. This was business, business, *business*.

Opening her eyes, she turned slowly to meet his. His vivid blue stare pinned her to where she stood and she nearly sucked back a startled breath. The clarity there, well that was certainly a new attribute she hadn't expected to see.

"Hi."

He said the word easy enough, but the way he swallowed hard while stuffing his hands in his jeans pockets and shifting his stance from foot to foot said something completely different. He was sober—and uncomfortable.

Interesting.

There wasn't a hint of a slur in his voice, not a drunken droop to his eyelids or the pallor of a hangover to his skin as he stared her down from three feet away. She'd heard rumors he'd cleaned up, but she had to admit she never believed one word of it.

Even with the proof right in front her, she still couldn't respond. She wanted to, really she did, if for nothing else than to keep the upper hand. But she couldn't. Instead she simply stared back—at his wide and lightly tanned bare chest, at his drool-worthy abs and the fine trail of hair that disappeared to happier places beyond his waistband. Her gaze reversed direction then and traveled up beyond all that to a set of killer shoulders—those same muscular shoulders she'd clutched so many times, arching into him those final seconds before coming apart under him.

His neck was tapered and strong, his jaw uncharacteristically scruffy with a perfectly trimmed five o'clock shadow. But when she looked higher and took in those full lips as the edge lifted in a knowing grin, that was when he blew it.

Oh, hell no—the cocky son of a bitch. She met his gaze for a heated second with the intent of driving daggers into his skull before she spun around and stormed off. She needed to get away—far away from that smug smirk on his lips and the heartbreaking memories that seeing him in the flesh made flood back.

But more than that, she needed to get away from the way he always made her feel.

Uncontrolled. Wild.

And—Lord help her—so much like a goddamned fool.

Chapter Two

Ah, shit! Well, that didn't pan out the way he'd hoped. Ryan completely bombed at trying to pull off that casual "Hey, there. Remember me? Your ex-lover?" look. As an actor, he could've nailed the steamy gaze in a heartbeat, but him just trying to be himself? Apparently not so much.

"Brynn, wait!" He jogged a few steps until he caught up to her, but she held up her hand to ward him off.

"Don't. Don't speak to me, don't even look at me."

He grasped her elbow and pulled her to a stop, well aware of the questioning stares from the crew as their little tête-à-tête started to draw attention. She looked down at his hand and back up to his face before twisting her arm out of his grip.

"And you certainly can't touch me."

"Wait, please. Just give me five minutes. I need to talk to you." When she didn't answer, he reiterated. "Come on. Just five minutes."

"I don't have anything to say to you."

He sighed. Sure, he'd known this wasn't going to be easy. Hell, what had he expected? For her to jump on him, wrap her arms and legs around him as she covered his face with kisses and pledged her undying love? No, not hardly. But he had to remain cool and composed in the face of her indignation. One slip-up, one little glimpse of the man he used to be and it'd be game over. And he wanted to prove to her, more than anything else, that he was different now, that he wasn't even close to the man he was six months ago.

"Let me do the talking. Give me the chance to say all the things I should've said before."

She shook her head. Her eyes were filled with a crushing anger and bitter pain while her breaths came out short and strangled. "It's too late for anything you have to tell me."

He stepped closer and she folded her arms over her breasts and averted her eyes, effectively shutting him out. Unwilling to let her dismiss him so easily, he distracted her by tracing along her arm with a gentle finger while he lifted her chin with another. Her skin was so warm. Soft. God, he missed how amazing she always felt. "Don't say that. It's never too late."

The words barely left his lips before she was retreating. "It was too late that night, and it's too late now. Why you, anyway? Why are you here?"

The lift of one shoulder led to an easy, "Same as you, probably. I need this movie. We need it."

Another snippet of her resentment rose to the surface. "Don't lump us together, Ryan. You don't know anything about me anymore."

And yeah, she was right about that. But even though they hadn't seen each other in quite a while, he was still taken aback by that connection. That primal way they reacted to each other. They simply sizzled together, there was no other way to describe it.

Man, he wanted to kick his own ass for the shitty situation he forced them to be in. But it was a situation he could repair, one he desperately *wanted* to repair, if only she'd give him the chance to apologize.

The PA passed by in a flurry of clipboard notes and walkie-talkie ramblings. "Ten minutes, folks. If we could get you on set, please?"

Ryan cringed at the visible panic rising inside her as all the color drained from her face.

"No. No, I can't. Not with him."

The assistant paused mid-stride and backpedaled a step or two before his beady gaze bounced a bit too harshly between the two of them. "Excuse me? Is there a problem? Should I call over the AD? The director?"

She paused a moment with her mouth open, as if contemplating the underlying threat the little weasel just made. Leave it to this clock-watching perfectionist to play a dirty hand, but score one for the punk, too. When she finally answered, Ryan let out the breath he hadn't realized he'd been holding.

"Sorry, no. No problem."

"Good. In ten, then?"

Brynn pasted on the sweetest, fakest smile Ryan had ever seen.

"Fine," she remarked as the PA hurried away. In the next breath, she turned and pierced Ryan with a steely glare. "I'll do this," she said, her voice lowered. "But only because of my commitment to this picture and because of my contract. This is a simple love scene between our characters. It doesn't have a thing to do with us, but has *everything* to do with my career. I'm sure you could have a flock of starlets groveling at your feet willing to do a scene like this with you, but believe me when I say I'm not one of them.

"I'm a professional and a damn good actress, and yes, I *need* this movie. I swear to God though, if you cross the line, if you do *anything* to mess this up for me..." She threw the next words at him with a stark vehemence. "The shitstorm you created in my life six months ago? I'll flip that around so fast, what happened will seem like a walk in the park to what I'll put you through. That, Mr. Manning, is a promise." And with a hitch of her chin, she bolted away from him and headed toward the set.

Ryan stood there, stunned. But he couldn't help himself—he actually grinned as she swished that cute little backside further away from him. He grinned at her vigor, at the verve with which she clearly spoke each word. They were hate-filled, but still.

Her hatred he could deal with. He expected it. What he couldn't deal with, what caused him the most concern, was that not-so-gentle reminder of the pain he'd inflicted on her. A pain he now had to wash away, thoroughly and quickly if he was going to move forward with her.

And beyond all else, now that he'd seen and touched her again, now that he'd gotten another glimpse of that spark within her, that's what he wanted most. Despite her bitterness, despite her harsh words, he was going to find a way to make everything up to her. After years of darkness, of self-hatred and even more self-destruction, he was finally ready to move forward into a new and better life. Come hell or high water, he was going to do that.

And he was damn sure going to do it with Brynn.

* * * * *

Brynn spotted Roman waiting for her by the bed on set with a powder puff in hand and a grim expression on his face. Furious tears over her encounter with Ryan threatened to spill, but she held them back, determined not to crash in front of everyone around her and make a spectacle of herself. Roman motioned her over just as the assistant made the announcement indicating they were ready to begin.

"All nonessential personnel please clear the set."

This was it. The one scene in the entire movie that had given her any doubt, and now she'd be filming it with the one man who held the power to break her concentration, let alone her heart.

"Do you believe in destiny?" Roman asked when she got closer.

"Don't start with me, please."

She dropped the robe past her shoulders, still clutching the edges together over her breasts. She wasn't quite ready to get naked in front of the crew, or Ryan either for that matter. Roman dabbed the final touches of sheer powder along her shoulders, then knelt to work on her legs. He flicked a glance up at her before returning his attention to the job at hand. "I'm just saying, Ryan Manning? With the history you two have?"

"Roman, for heaven's sake, there is no history. We got lost in each other a few times." Huh, more than a *few* times. "Nothing ever came of it."

Nothing ever could. Ryan had always gotten too wasted as their "dates" went on, had been too thoughtless. They'd driven each other crazy for three months straight before that final night, before Ryan's careless actions and even crueler words sealed the deal for her. As much as she loved the kind man he could be during the light of day, she hated the man who appeared once night fell and the serious drinking began.

"Oh, you two have a history all right. Or have you forgotten all about last summer?"

Up to now, she'd tried. She'd tried hard to forget everything about Ryan Manning. About the way he touched her. His easy dominance. And the way she could fall under his control in a heartbeat.

Damn him for showing up here. Damn him for throwing her off-kilter like this. And double damn him for looking better than he ever had before.

Yeah, she'd noticed, despite his cocky smirk, despite her anger. But what she didn't understand was the *why* of it all. Why now? Why here? But more to the point, why on earth did she react so strongly to him?

She knew lots of gorgeous actors. In this business they were a dime a dozen. He certainly wasn't special in that area. So what made him so freaking different from everyone else?

"No, Roman, I haven't forgotten. As much as I've tried, Lord knows I haven't."

"So what now?"

That was the million dollar question, wasn't it? "You know what they say, the show must go on." She let out a derisive chuckle. "Unless I shoot myself first."

Roman stood and fiddled with her hair. "I still think it all goes back to destiny." He looked at her then with that big-brother protectiveness, albeit laced with an evil smile. "But even so, all you have to do is say the word, hon. You know I have connections."

Scary thought, that. "Thanks, but I don't think that'll be necessary. I can handle it."

At least she hoped she could.

Roman squeezed her shoulder and stepped off set just as Ryan came on. His upper body was now covered with a torn and tattered button-down shirt, and his makeup artist had spiked up his hair into a sexy wind-blown look. He moved into the hallway of the set's apartment, and with a deep breath and one final look in her eyes, he closed the door with him on the other side.

A zing of heat from that single look alone shot past her anger, and her entire body blazed from the inside out. So much for the *never let 'em see you sweat* adage, she mused, curbing the urge to fan herself with her fingers to try to cool off.

Lord, she hoped to hell and back that she'd be able to pull this off.

The scene had very little dialogue, thank goodness. It was mostly a reunion of their characters after a night of the heroine worrying about her cop boyfriend, the hero. Brynn's character, a headstrong gallery owner, was to be woken by him in the middle of the night after he'd left a romantic dinner with her earlier to chase down the bad guys.

She scooted onto the bed and cursed as the modesty patch between her legs shifted. Sweat and sticky tape certainly didn't mix well, and she discreetly pressed the patch back in place and pulled up the covers before slinking out of the robe and tossing it to a stagehand. The silkiness of the sheets slid over her damp skin, and the sensuality of the cool fabric only added to the electricity already firing through her system.

The PA called out to the remaining crew. "Okay people, here we go. Quiet on the set."

With multiple cameras in place, she prayed they'd get this in one shot. For sanity's sake—hers—they had to.

"Places, please," the PA ordered.

Brynn rolled to her side, faced away from cameras and waited.

"And action!"

The snick of the door opening was her cue. She peered over her shoulder just as Ryan—no, damn it! Not Ryan. She couldn't think of him out of character. Not now. He was Dan Taylor, homicide detective. He had to be.

But that wasn't Dan looking at her like that now. That was all Ryan. Fiery and blatantly sexual. She swallowed, hard.

"You're back," she said.

"I told you I would be."

She shifted and held the sheet over her breasts. The feel of her nipples poking through made her hate the way her body betrayed her. But, damn him again, he'd always had that effect on her. "I wasn't so sure you'd make it."

"I'll always come back to you. I made that promise. I have every intention of keeping it." He moved closer to the bed. "If you'll let me."

This was the part where she was supposed to drop the sheet. She mentally sucked in a breath, battered down her trepidation and chanted over and over in her head that she was a professional actress. She could do this. She *had* to do this.

Yep. Okay. Here we go…

"Yes, Dan. Yes." And there went the sheet.

A spark flared in Ryan's eyes and his jaw ticked as he pulled the remnants of the shirt off to reveal that luscious chest of his. Her throat went dry, and she told herself it wasn't because she still wanted him, still wanted his touch, but only because of raw nerves. It had to be. She simply couldn't deal with any other reason.

But then he moved over her and laid her back on the bed. The heat coming off his skin… Dear God. He wrapped her in his arms and worked his hands under her back while she in turn wrapped hers around his neck. They stayed like that a moment, in a familiar embrace, with him staring in her eyes and her trying her damnedest to read beyond his character to what Ryan was really feeling.

The edge of his lip lifted again, but it was different this time. He was different. Even in the dim lighting needed for this scene, the brightness in his eyes surprised her. He was all here, focused. Determined. He looked so damn sincere.

The thought had her head spinning. No, she had to be reading more into his expression than was really there. This was just him acting. Ryan would never change. He'd always be the same selfish jerk he was back then.

Oh, but what if…

"I'm sorry I worried you. I'm so sorry about a lot of things." And then he kissed her.

No, God no. It had to be Dan who kissed her. With passion and caring and everything sexy a kiss should be. But all she tasted was Ryan. Only this time the flavor was that of a rich coffee laced with a subtle hint of chocolate. There wasn't a trace of gin or whiskey or any other alcohol to be found. He tasted sweet and strong, and despite their history, despite everything he'd put her through, the combination drove her absolutely out of her mind.

Trevor had lied. He had *so* lied. Nothing about this was technical. This was hot—blazing hot. And completely unexpected.

Yes, the cameras were there. Yes, they were being watched by more than a few dozen complete strangers. But she couldn't seem to care. With a single touch of his lips to hers, Ryan had somehow forced everything around them to fade away into a murky haze. The set, the lights and all the people. She knew they were there, but it didn't matter. Right here, right now, nothing mattered. Nothing but the two of them.

He'd transported her away from reality, to a time that once could've been. She was caught in the moment, in his kiss, in a crazy rush of what-if's and never-got-to-be's. She'd been held by him like this before, many times, and the ache for the feeling had never completely gone away. She needed this from him, his gentle yet commanding grip, the way he always took charge of her passion.

He pressed his hips into hers and she melted at the feel of his erection, hard and thick behind the zipper of his jeans. He wanted her. There was nothing fake about what was going on between them. And, Lord have mercy, she couldn't help herself, she moved against him—*with* him—raising her knees and cocooning him in the vee of her thighs.

A groan rose from his chest as he left her lips to kiss along her chin. He traveled lower, nipping and biting the sensitive tendon along her neck. Turning her head, she opened herself to him. To his soft mouth, to his sharp teeth. It all felt so good. *He* felt so good.

He cupped her breast then as she ran her fingers through his hair, arching her back a little as she did so.

She wasn't acting anymore either. This was all her, and she loved it. Loved being in his arms again, loved the softness of the denim covering his ass as she dug her heels in to hold him there. Loved the tickle of his chest hair against her abdomen as he moved, going lower, *yes*, lower. And she especially loved the burn of his lips when he took her nipple into his mouth.

As a sparkle of pleasure tore straight through her, she lifted her head to nuzzle his hair and breathed in that well-known sexy scent of sandalwood and spice. Her body throbbed and her fingers tightened a little more around the short, spiky strands.

He slicked kisses along the rise of her breast to her shoulder and ground harder against her. They moved together in a singular motion—her under him in a daze of sudden need, him over her with an expression of determination and desire. They kissed, clutched, moaned. His hands gripped her hips now, and she released his hair to cling to his shoulders like she'd done so many times before. He rocked them gently to their sides, but something wicked inside her took over. She pushed him all the way until he lay on his back and she straddled his thighs.

In her mind's eye she saw the fluid choreography and the way they looked so natural together. So beautiful, so in sync. God, they always had.

She unfastened his jeans and reared back along his legs while he lifted his ass. As she yanked his pants past his hips, she had to bite back a groan. The modesty patch he wore barely hid even half of him. The ridiculous things sure as hell weren't made for a man with an erection, and certainly not an erection as impressive as this one.

His beautiful cock burst past the end of the patch to lay long and hard over his pelvis, and Brynn had to take a moment to remind herself they weren't filming a porno here and knew that most of this scene, anything in-your-face and blatant, would more than likely end up on the cutting room floor. But regardless of that knowledge, a little part of her wanted to take that proverbial extra step and move up just a little so she could slide back over him. Lord, how she wanted him inside her again.

Instead, she tried her hardest to ignore his cock and crawled up his body, biting her lip at the same time so she wouldn't lean down and lick that gorgeous swollen head, or take the rest of his length deep into her mouth. He'd always loved it when she went down on him, had loved fisting the hair at her nape as he controlled her every thrust, all the while watching intently. The hair at the back of her neck stood out as if it craved the familiar pull, the harsh way he used to grip her. But then he lifted his arms over his head. The action distracted her and she got lost in the stretch of his upper body, in the defined ridges of his abdomen and the tiny peaks in the center of his flat, brown nipples. She bit her lip a little harder.

He was breathtaking lying under her like this. And she'd give anything to possess enough carelessness to throw all caution to the wind. She was beyond turned on now, drowning in an overload of touches, feelings and ancient memories, and as soon as she settled herself astride him again, he had to have known it too. Her pussy was hot, so wet. So damn ready. They both momentarily closed their eyes when she shifted her hips and rubbed over him. It was such a tiny move, just a little wriggle, but enough of one to have them both gasping for breath. His nostrils flared and his chest expanded on a deep inhale.

After a hard swallow, he clenched his jaw and whispered, "Take from me. Take what you want."

Oh, shit. Lines. But wait, there wasn't supposed to be any dialogue during this part, only at the beginning. With her hands on his chest, she propped herself up and stared into his eyes.

No, he wasn't reciting any sort of lines. He was talking to her, the *real* her. She could see it in his gaze. Her body felt on fire and she knew right then there was no turning back. Film, no film, anger, hurt, embarrassment—none of that came into play, not anymore. Her body was speaking for her, as it always had whenever she found herself in his arms. They were connected on some sort of twisted level she didn't understand, one she wasn't even remotely ready to grasp. And deep down, she knew she should hate him for it.

But she was too far gone and her body didn't care, not one iota. It instinctively knew what to do, and as she began to move over him in a fake act of movie-making fucking, he gripped her hips and helped her along. The adhesive on the patches didn't stand a chance against the moisture they created between them, and both pieces of thin material slipped further and further away with each frantic movement. In a flash they were bare. Nothing could stop the wicked shiver racking her body at the sudden fiery skin-on-skin contact or the hiss of her indrawn breath as her uncovered clit rubbed along his length with every phony thrust. Swirling tingles began to build low in her belly as her nipples tightened to painful little buds. She moaned, because God, she couldn't help it. But when he did too, that's when she knew it was too late.

She gripped his biceps and dug her fingernails into the muscles there while his hips and thighs flexed and stiffened under her. Their stares met and she swore, regardless of the din of their heavy breathing, that she heard him growl.

"That's it, baby. That's it. Let go. God, just let go."

An unexpected, fierce orgasm bulldozed over her the precise instant one of the worst memories of her life rushed back full throttle. A memory of him, at the after-party for the premiere of his latest movie, drunk as a skunk and fucking a younger clone of herself in the hotel's coat closet.

And goddamn him if he hadn't slurred those same words—those same *exact* words—to the young starlet he'd been ramming into from behind.

Chapter Three

Ryan knew the instant he fucked up. He didn't know exactly what he'd done, but the tortured look on Brynn's face said it all.

Christ, when was he ever going to get it right with her?

She waited a heartbeat after the AD said, "Um, cut?" before slapping him hard across the face. He dug his fingers into the soft flesh at her hips as his head flew to the side and stars glittered behind his closed eyes. Wow, she had one hell of an arm on her.

She shimmied to get out of his hold, and even though he knew he should let go, he gripped her tighter. She'd come, but he hadn't. And even with the knowledge that he'd once again done *something* wrong, he was right there on the verge of exploding. Another little move like that and he'd not only embarrass himself, but he'd for sure make her angrier.

"Let go of me, you bastard," she said through gritted teeth.

He opened and closed his mouth to work out the throb in his jaw. "One second. Just give me one damn second," he said in a lame attempt to buy himself a little time to calm down. His body was still on fire and, Jesus, the way she was moving on him trying to get away was killing him. But when he met her angry stare a moment later, the raw pain in her eyes attacked him and served as a cold, wet blanket for his libido.

"I'm sure I did something to deserve that, but hell, Brynn."

"Let. Go. Of. Me."

The prick he used to be would've said "Screw it" and kept his hands on her just for spite. But the new Ryan hated the anguish in her voice and hated even more being the cause of it. So he let go and reached for the crumpled sheet at his side, but she snatched it away before he had the chance to act gentlemanly and hand it to her. She wrapped it around herself and clambered off him and out of the bed in such a hurry she nearly fell over the side doing so.

She clearly couldn't get away from him fast enough.

He sat up in the bed and offered her his hand as everyone else on set was either pretending to be busy or blatantly gaping at them, all slack-jawed and engrossed in the drama that seemed to surround the two of them whenever they came together.

"Brynn, damn it, hold on just a minute. We need to talk."

She ignored him and instead clutched the sheet tighter over her breasts, hung her head and bolted for the stage door.

On a foul-mouthed curse, he grabbed his jeans from the floor and stood to punch a foot through the right pant leg only to end up hopping around like a fool and nearly falling himself, at the same time trying to get his left leg in and not lose sight of her as she ran away. He knew he looked like an idiot, but he didn't care. He had to get to her, had to make her see that what just happened, how they reacted to each other, well it was… *Right* might sound almost pretentious and a little corny, but nothing else described it better, not for him.

Her orgasm had surprised him just as much as it apparently surprised her. Was that what got her mad? He sure as hell didn't understand if it was. He loved it, every second of it. Why would something that felt so right get her so pissed?

Because it all goes back to the way she hates you, you stupid ass.

Hell, maybe he *was* crazy thinking she'd accept him now. She probably thought some sort of subterfuge on his part led to him getting on this movie. Something sneaky and underhanded. And yeah, at one time he wouldn't have thought twice about using or abusing anyone or anything to get what he wanted.

But not this time. Just because circumstances and timing couldn't have been better, he still *earned* his part in this movie.

And now he had to earn back Brynn's trust.

He took off and followed after her but shit, she moved fast. She was practically running by the time he caught sight of her outside the sound stage doors heading toward a row of dressing-room trailers. He caught up with her just in time to get a trailer door slammed in his face.

Not giving her the chance to flip the lock, he yanked on the handle and hopped up the last step into the trailer. She was still clutching the sheet over her breasts and held a hand over her mouth as she spun away from him.

When he closed the door with a quiet click, she flung the hand from her mouth and lifted her face to the ceiling. "Why! Why are you doing this to me?"

"Brynn," he said and stepped closer.

She whirled on him with fire blazing in her eyes. A fire that at one time could've been construed as sensual, but after what just happened, he'd have to vote for hatred instead.

"I was fine. Perfectly fine. Living my life the way I wanted, finally forgetting everything you put me through. And then you waltz in and decide to play head games with me." A single tear slid down her cheek and she swatted it away. "I want you to leave. You *have* to leave. *Now*."

He took another step toward her and barely had time to duck before she grabbed a small vase from the table behind her and launched it at him. It shattered against the wall over his shoulder and sprayed chunks of broken glass and dripping wet rose petals all around him.

"God, will you just go!"

She stood there in front of him with her fist clenched in that sheet, on the verge of panting and very definitely seething. When another furious tear escaped, his insides bunched tighter. Jesus, maybe he should leave and give her some time. Time to calm down and get over the shock of him being back. But if he did…

No, he wouldn't—*couldn't*—leave without clearing things up first.

"All I want is a chance to explain. To apologize."

That earned him an evil, sardonic laugh. "Apologize?"

"Brynn, so much has changed. I've changed." He took another guarded step. "Just sit down and listen."

"You put me through hell for months. *Months*, Ryan. And now I finally have a decent shot at improving not only my career but my life as well, and you just nonchalantly show up. Tell me, did you come here out of some sick thrill? Just to throw those same, cruel words in my face again? I guess once just wasn't enough for you, was it?"

Words? What words? Oh fuck, what had he said?

"Believe me when I say I'm sorry, Brynn, but I honestly don't know what you're talking about."

She squeezed her eyes shut as the tip of her nose turned a darker shade of pink. But it was the indrawn breath and the turn of her head with her lips pressed between her teeth that had him in a panic. Good God, even her chin was quivering.

She blew out her held breath and opened her eyes a moment later, a bit more unnaturally calm. And that freaked him the hell out.

"Yeah, I don't suppose you'd remember that, would you?" She chuckled again, but there was no humor in either the sound or in her eyes. "Doesn't that just figure."

"Brynn, please. Just tell me what I did."

Her eyes widened and she pitched forward slightly like she wanted to slap him again. "God, what *didn't* you do!"

He leaned back a little and rubbed along the nape of his neck to batter down the frustration creeping up inside him.

Shit, he could easily remember a time when he'd say "Fuck it" to having a conversation like this and instead rally a bunch of guys to head over to the nearest bar or go it alone to the closest liquor store. A fifth of vodka here, a bottle of scotch there, hell, it didn't matter. He'd chug down whatever he could get his hands on. It'd taken a good long while before the message penetrated his thick skull that drowning himself in booze had never solved a damn thing, that it never would.

"Okay, I deserve that, too. But Brynn, come on, you're not listening. All I'm asking for is a chance—"

"A chance to what? To drive me crazy?" She spun around again, forked a hand through her hair and stared out the trailer window. "Well, guess what, hotshot. Your plan's working like a charm."

Moving up behind her probably wasn't a good idea, but at this point he figured *anything* he tried wouldn't be a good idea in her eyes anyway. He came within mere inches of touching her, so close he could make out the tiniest freckles along her shoulders. He wanted to run his finger along those tiny brown patches, to play a sensual game of connect-the-dots all over her soft skin.

He had to clench his hands so he wouldn't.

The way she shivered and the goose bumps rising along her neck and down her back told him she felt both his presence and the breaths that always became hot and heavy whenever they were close. But even that reaction didn't stop her from telling him she didn't want him near.

"Just go, Ryan. I need this movie. I need it for me. For my career. And there's no way in hell I can do it with you around. You're just too much for me to deal with right now."

Yeah, he should do as she asked and leave. He was only causing her additional pain, and the very idea of that killed him even more. But he couldn't give up just yet. He needed to push just a bit further.

"I was in bad shape for a really long time, Brynn." He breathed the words at the edge of her ear, still not touching her even though everything inside him was dying to. He got a heady rush when she shivered again. "I'm not making excuses, not anymore. I made horrible choices, ones that hurt so many people. Ones that hurt you. If I could, I'd take it all back."

"Ryan. Stop."

"But there's one thing I'd never change," he said anyway. "I'd never change the way we were together." He stepped closer and his chest brushed against her back while his heart hammered and his blood raced through his veins. And this time, he didn't hold back from touching her.

Her shoulders bunched the instant he gripped her upper arms, but she didn't move away or try to twist from his hold, thank God. Not that he could've stopped her or even moved his own body. Her skin seared his palms, and all he *could* do was suck in a breath and grip her harder.

"You want to talk crazy? That was me every time I was around you. You drove me insane from how much I wanted you. I never could get enough."

"Please don't do this," she whispered.

"I remember the way we couldn't keep our hands off each other. All the afternoons we spent lying in bed just talking. Touching. That trip to the beach where we grilled shrimp on that tiny hibachi and later made love behind the sand dunes. Or the hour-long bath we took afterward and how much I loved soaping every inch of your body." He pushed gently against her ass, knowing he could very well be pushing her too far as well. "You feel that, baby? That's me remembering all of it. That's me wanting you more now than I ever did before."

She hung her head before releasing the tense set of her arms and quietly turning within his grip. Tears welled in her eyes, and even though he still touched her, the temperature of her skin had somehow cooled a degree or two.

"What you remember are all the good parts, Ryan." Her irises darkened to a deeper blue as one more lone tear spilled over. "Yet you don't know why what you said to me on set has me so mad. You don't even have a clue. That has me wondering then, do you even remember that last night we were together? Do you remember any part of it?"

Not giving him the chance to respond, she forged ahead. "Because I do. I remember every minute of it. How I caught you in that coat closet with your pants barely past your ass and how you had that girl bent over with her arms braced against the wall."

"Oh fuck," he mumbled. "Brynn…"

"But what I really remember," she went on while more tears fell, "was the way you slurred to her, 'I love you, Brynn. That's it, baby. That's it. Let go. God, just let go.'"

All the blood drained from his head as a sickening punch blasted his gut. Shit, he suddenly wanted to throw up.

She took a subtle step back out of his reach. "So you see, that's why I won't listen. I don't want to hear any of what you have to say. I've lived with those memories for so long that there isn't really anything you could tell me that would make it better anyway." She paused a minute, then moved to walk past him, but stopped at his side before she did. "I'm asking you one last time to leave, Ryan. Please. If you ever really cared for me at all, you'll just leave."

As he turned and watched her tiptoe around the glass and out the door, his mind reeled and he hated himself more than he ever had. He despised how much he'd scarred her, how deeply her wounds ran. Yet something inside him clutched to the knowledge that even the deepest, darkest scars were able to fade with enough time and healing.

And that alone made up his mind.

Nobody could make this right but him. Only he had the power to make damn sure Brynn Lang's scars healed. That they disappeared.

And that they disappeared *forever*.

Now he just had to figure out how the hell to do it.

Chapter Four

The end of the day hadn't come soon enough.

Even the twenty minute shower Brynn had taken hadn't put the slightest dent in making her feel any better. Now wrapped in a bath towel, she curled her legs underneath her on the couch in the resort's suite and sipped gingerly on a glass of chardonnay, giving herself a few blessed minutes of solitude before she finished getting ready for tonight's cast party.

After her conversation with Ryan, she felt completely out of sorts. Raw. Jittery. Every muscle ached. Christ, even her hair hurt.

The DVD with the dailies had been delivered earlier and it now sat on the coffee table in front of her. She stared at it, hoping it would spontaneously burst into a ball of flames and take away the option of her being able to watch it.

The raw footage of her and Ryan was on that thing, and she wished it would burn for that very reason. The last thing she wanted was to relive what happened this morning.

Although, in reality, she'd been reliving it all damn day. Even now her face felt flushed and a wicked trail tingled up her thighs and spread into her pussy. So she gave in a bit too easily and set her wineglass down only to snatch up the DVD. She stalked over to the desk and shoved the disc none too gently into the drive on her laptop before flopping onto the leather chair and crossing her arms and legs in a huff to wait for it to boot up.

She dealt with the first moments of the scene setup easily enough, but when "action" was called and Ryan opened the set's door, her stomach dropped like a stone. He simply took over the screen, embodied it with a kind of charisma found in only the rarest of actors.

Figures. The flipping bastard.

And it only got worse. She had to look away at the part where he kissed her. She couldn't handle remembering the bright, savory way he tasted or how his hard muscles felt like boulders under her hands. But when a sultry moan sounded through the tinny speakers of her computer, she had to look back.

Oh God, that was *her* moaning.

She bolted upright in the chair and slapped the laptop closed. It only took another second before she hopped up and paced around the room. Her insides were skittering about, raging an untimely war and making her feel like she wanted to jump clean out of her skin.

He said he'd changed. And really, who was she to say he hadn't? He could've, it'd been done before. Millions of people had sobered up and moved on with their lives. Hadn't they?

Could he be one of them?

The what if's killed her. What if he was lying to her? What if he really hadn't quit drinking? But on the flip side, what if he really *had*? What if he'd done a complete one-eighty and ditched the booze for a sober lifestyle?

She picked up her wineglass on a swing by the coffee table before continuing her pace to the sliding glass doors of the suite's private balcony. She had, of course, been assigned a beach-accessible room, but even the bright pinks and purples of the dusky sky just beginning to edge across the water didn't do a damn thing to help calm her.

A couple holding hands strolled along the edge of the surf, soaking in the last remnants of daylight while a woman and her dog jogged around them and headed further down the beach. But it was the man sitting in the sand halfway between the resort and the water who snagged her attention.

She'd know that powerfully built frame anywhere. How his neck sloped into those shoulders, and how those shoulders gave way to a pair of thick, muscular arms. Arms that now rested on his knees as he stared into the ocean.

Her heart ached as she watched Ryan, and as she went to take a sip of her wine, she ended up studying the gold liquid sloshing around inside the glass instead.

If it hadn't been for Ryan's love of alcohol and the unpleasantness that resulted because of it, she knew in her heart she'd still be with him. They'd clicked the instant they met at a star-studded charity fundraiser and had been inseparable the rest of the summer. God, they'd laughed together so much. Loved together. At least during the day.

His drinking had started out casually enough, but then morphed bit by bit into a freak parade she never saw coming. It wasn't as if she were some sort of teetotaler herself. Hell, at the beginning she'd almost given him a run for his money. They often split a bottle of wine, sometimes two, when they went out for dinner. Strange how—at the time—a couple cocktails seemed to heighten their desire. The resulting sex had been off the charts and had easily lasted for hours. But as those lazy days of summer spanned into a longer trail of harried weeks, he'd ended up getting more and more smashed.

A pattern had somehow formed. One she didn't understand and really didn't want to be a part of anymore. Most nights she tried to ignore the steady progression and would placate him with a few kisses or strokes before tucking him into bed. She'd often curl up faced away from him, nursing a deep pang of longing he'd yet again left unfulfilled.

But he never failed to wake next to her in the morning, gather her in his arms to apologize with such a beautiful sincerity before making love to her so slowly and sweetly that she had no other choice but to melt under him, or to believe him with all her heart.

Christ, that happened so many times.

With a weary breath, she traipsed to the bathroom and poured the wine down the drain. The fruity sweetness—or more likely those difficult memories—had suddenly turned her stomach sour. Besides, the wine only represented everything that had gone wrong in her life. It was time for her to move forward, time for her to move past all that. She brushed her teeth to rid her mouth of the flavor before shedding the towel and reaching for her hairbrush.

As she blew her hair dry, restless thoughts bombarded her mind. It didn't seem fair that one of the worst nights for her could end up changing Ryan's life for the better. Seeing him like that, wasted and fucking that girl, had killed her inside. And as he spouted those three little words to the tramp in the coat closet, it struck her that he'd never told her he loved her before. What made him say it then? What made that time so different?

Her mother had a favorite saying, one that if she let her heart open just a little, could be fairly apropos now—*A drunken man's words were a sober man's thoughts.*

Had he really loved her? If he had, he should've had the cojones to tell her when he was sober. That he didn't said so much.

She yanked the brush through her hair, getting angrier at not just him, but herself as well. Christ, she sounded so sanctimonious. He should've done this, he should've done that. But when it came right down to it, what had she done?

Would things have turned out differently if she'd stepped forward and mentioned his excessive drinking and how it worried her? What would've happened if she'd found the nerve to say *I love you* first? And really, why hadn't she?

As she stood there staring at her reflection in the mirror, all the reasons—rational or otherwise—created havoc in her soul.

Time, for them, had always rushed by in a chaotic whirlwind. But more than being caught in some sort of erotic undertow, the romantic in her *wanted* that fairy tale, wanted the hot actor that fans drooled over to sweep her off her feet. And he had at first. Their compatibility and similarities ran so deep. It amazed her that she'd finally done it, she'd finally found her dream man—the one with the controlled dominant side, the one who could make her wet with a single look, and the one who could make her laugh with the stupidest joke. She knew, deep down, that he'd choose the perfect moment to tell her he loved her, and when he did, the heavens would open, harps would play and a choir of angels would sing…

Yeah, right. Not.

So she'd held her tongue about all the other stuff and clung to the idea that he was just working through a difficult phase in his life. He'd stop all the bullshit drinking, right?

Apparently not until he'd broken her heart, damn him.

She tossed the hairdryer and brush onto the bathroom counter and grabbed her makeup case. She'd given up on her personal pity parties months ago, so she needed to put the kibosh on the one creeping up on her now. Anger so often worked better for her, anyway.

Trying to steady her suddenly shaky hand, she took a deep breath and applied a thin layer of eyeliner along with a few swoops of mascara. It wasn't as if she had anybody to get dolled up for tonight and had originally planned on making just a quick appearance at the cast party before getting the hell out of Dodge, but something inside her now wanted to dress to impress. Or dress to make jealous.

Okay, that sounded petty, but who cared? She was tired of wallowing, tired of giving others the upper hand. And damn tired of wanting him so badly she was ready to scream.

Even now her body still burned for him. Lord, maybe he really *was* driving her crazy.

After applying a little blush and layering on the perfect shades of lip gloss, she fluffed her hair, slipped into a tiny strap of a thong and grabbed the dress hanging from the hook on the door. A cute halter number, the deep cleavage and lacy black material would surely be enough to have the guys ogling her.

Still petty, but what the hell.

She headed back to the main room, grabbing her favorite pair of strappy heels and snatching up her room key on her way through before flipping the light off and dousing the suite in darkness.

Was Ryan still on the beach? Since the party was being held by the pool, she could easily leave through the balcony door to get there and pass by with a sultry sashay to let him have a good look at what he'd been missing out on. Teasing was mean, but again, what the hell. He deserved it.

Just as she got to the balcony door, Ryan was rising to stand. He was dressed casually, in a pair of dark jeans and a white short-sleeved button down shirt that practically glowed in the dusk's radiant twilight. She swallowed hard at how form-fitting the shirt was and how it showed off the wide expanse of his back all the way down to the gentle taper of his waist.

A flutter raced through her pussy, but by now she'd come to expect the primal need he created whenever she laid eyes on him. Giving herself a little erotic leeway, she soaked in the sight of his tight butt in those jeans as he brushed away the sand, and then scanned lower—past his rock-hard thighs and calves and further on to his bare feet.

He planted his hands on his hips and kicked the sand around a little. He seemed so lonely standing out there, like he didn't know what to do with himself. Hell, maybe he really didn't.

Most habits die hard and to give up ones that, like it or not, defined you, well… Replacing them could be just as difficult as walking away from them in the first place, if not more so. If he *was* sober now, what had he substituted for the drinking? What took away the urge, curbed the craving?

If she had to guess from looking at him, she'd lay odds he'd thrown himself back into working out, maybe even picked up a weekend game or two of beach volleyball. He used to love playing, and his legs and shoulders looked as though they'd tightened up somewhat—if that were even possible. Besides, the tan he sported told her he'd spent some time in the sun lately. Just seeing him all golden reminded her of that Saturday at the beach he mentioned earlier. He'd gotten so sweaty after a raucous game he and a few others had played in the blazing midday sun. So much like that scene in *Top Gun,* only ten times better. And later they'd messed around with that damn hibachi for a good twenty minutes before they finally got it started. The shrimp was so succulent, as was he afterward when they fooled around on the other side of the sand dune.

A miserable knot rose up and crowded out her ire to catch in her throat at the memory. God, she hated to admit how much she really did miss him. All the happy times. The private, goofy jokes they shared all the way down to the ferocious, dominant way he made love to her.

That she missed him so much tore her up inside. He'd *cheated* on her for God's sake, had screwed another woman in public for anyone to see, for *her* to see—never mind the fact he'd called the woman *Brynn* and had slurred his undying love to the little bitch.

Had fate been with her that day?

In that she'd been the only one to see him with that bimbo, maybe. But once he'd lifted those droopy eyelids and seen her from across the coat closet only to realize it wasn't her he was fucking, his shouts had drawn plenty of attention from not just the premiere attendees but from the hotel staff and other guests as well. He'd pushed the girl aside and raced after her, but she never looked back, not once. His panicked yells as she forced her way through the hotel's revolving door and out onto the sidewalk before scrambling into a cab hadn't even been enough to make her want to turn around.

As if he sensed those dismal memories, he glanced over his shoulder in the direction of her room. She didn't think he could see her, not in the dim light that surrounded her, but the way he stared a minute before turning his whole body had her wondering for sure. He took a step, then another and she found herself mimicking him and pressing her palms flat against the glass, in full view, when she could go no further. Her blood burned like fire through her veins and her head spun even faster.

She didn't want to believe him any more than she wanted to shove a red-hot poker in her eye. Because if she did, it would mean giving up her renewed anger. She needed it now, wholeheartedly relied on it to keep her focused. Even though the rush of heat tingling over her skin proved her body had no qualms in reacting to him, she hoped to hell and beyond that her heart and mind wouldn't be so easily conquered.

But then his expression changed, darkened somewhat. He lowered his shoulders and clenched his hands at his sides again and again while his chest expanded on a deep breath. And when he licked his lips, she flinched. A tiny, angry coil inside her snapped free and she gripped the door handle.

I shouldn't be doing this.

The thought popped in her mind, and she flat-out ignored it. It was the flash of instant need mixed with that draw, that fucking helpless draw that had her yanking the door open and stepping out onto the balcony as he ran up the steps two at a time. He came to a stop inches from her, breathing fast and hard, but so was she. With the last bit of sanity floating in her mind, she spun away, because God, she had to, but he grabbed her elbow in a tight grip before she could escape his reach. As he pulled her closer, the anticipation of a killer kiss tingled all the way to her toes. And as his lips crashed against hers, that weak expectation was blown completely out of the water. Every ounce of air whooshed from her lungs, but she couldn't find the means to care. He was kissing her, like he had so many times before, like he had that very morning.

Body, one. Heart and mind, zero.

"Brynn," he whispered against her lips as they clutched each other.

"Shut up," she replied, not wanting to think about what she was doing, or why. All she wanted was for him to touch her, for him to extinguish the blaze racing over her skin.

He bent his knees to pull her closer while he dipped his tongue into her mouth. He tasted much as he had earlier. Fresh, clean. New, yet so agonizingly familiar too. She'd never get over the way he held her in his arms, or the way he kissed the living hell out of her.

He cupped her ass, and she didn't wait for any sort of invitation. She dropped her sandals and room key, lifted to her toes and practically crawled up his body until she could wrap her legs around his hips. In a half-dozen steps, he had her pinned against the glass door.

Everything happened so fast. She couldn't think and it didn't matter. Her fingers found their way into his hair. His moved from her ass to caress along her thighs. When he lifted under her knees and rocked into her, she broke from the kiss and thumped her head back on the glass.

"Oh *God*."

He was so hard and thick, and she'd missed him so damn much. An inferno raged between them. Even their clothing didn't mute the fire where their bodies met.

As he kissed lower down her neck, she squeezed her eyes and turned her head. He was headed for that spot, that one little spot that always drove her out of her freaking mind. He found it in a heartbeat with his tongue, and she held back a throaty moan at the first hot, wet pass.

He had her upended, from not just the sheer pleasure as he licked, nipped and kissed her over and over, but from the fact he remembered how much she loved his mouth there in the first place.

And that only served to remind her of everything he *hadn't* remembered.

She fisted her hands in his hair and pulled his head away from her neck as another flare of anger hit her chest dead center. "Stop." Her body didn't want him to, but he *had* to. He groaned, fighting her, going for her neck again, and Christ she almost let him. "You have to *stop*, Ryan."

His steely gaze met hers with a mixture of pain and confusion. "No. Don't say that."

They were both breathing in short, strangled pants. She rested her forehead against his and tightened her fingers tangled in his hair. "I can't do this." Her skin was crying out for more of his touches and her heart felt like it was being ripped in two, but she had to keep her wits about her. No way could she let him suck her back in again.

She loosened her grip and trailed her fingertips down his neck. The power there enthralled her, but she had to keep going. She traced along his collarbones through the thin cotton of his shirt before stroking down to his pecs. With a push, she lifted her head. "Put me down."

He closed his eyes for a second before complying and gently lowering her to the balcony. The way his shoulders slumped before he turned away surprised her. She figured he'd explode, or try walking her down memory lane again to change her mind. But he didn't do either of those things. He simply laced his fingers behind his head with an agitated acceptance.

"Jesus, Brynn," he muttered.

"Yeah," she agreed.

"Tell me what you want me to do." He lowered his hands to his hips but kept his back to her. "Tell me how to make this right."

"Ryan."

He turned to face her. The pain in his eyes seemed so genuine, so goddamned real.

"There has to be something. I'll do anything, Brynn. I'll do anything to make you see how sorry I am."

The pounding of her heart beat hard against her arms as she crossed them over her breasts. Her very soul ached as the answer came all too easily. She picked up her shoes and the key and said, "There's nothing you can do, Ryan. Nothing you say will ever make this better."

And with those heart-wrenching words, she walked away from the only man she'd ever loved.

Chapter Five

Bullshit, there was nothing he could do. He could do plenty, but most of the ideas rolling around in his brain would probably go over like a lead balloon or end up with her slapping him again. Not that he really minded, but still.

After she walked away, he needed to hang back for a while. He was starting to lose patience with her and he didn't want her see him like that. He got that she was pissed and hurt beyond reason, but Jesus H. Christ… All he wanted was a chance, one lousy chance to explain, to tell her what he'd learned in rehab and to say what he should've said back then.

I love you.

But according to her, he'd already said those words, and he'd said them to the wrong person. Fuck, he wanted to punch a hole in the wall.

Had he been so much worse off that night than he'd originally thought? He remembered whispering in her ear that he had to take a leak, but of course, just *had* to slam down those two shots sitting on the table before he got up to leave. He weaved his way through the crowd and out into the hallway, hardly able to figure out which way he was supposed to go. He took a left and only made it a few steps when giggles bubbled from behind him and a set of arms slid around his waist. Before he knew what was happening, he was being pushed into the coat closet with his cock fisted in a warm hand.

God, he swore Brynn had been the one doing all that.

It was dark in there, or maybe he only thought it was because he couldn't keep his drunk-ass eyes open. When the woman dropped to her knees and took him into her mouth, he'd stopped her. He didn't want a blowjob, what he wanted was to fuck Brynn. He'd been dying to fuck her all night. The way she looked in that silver, strapless dress... Christ, he'd had a hard-on since she'd slipped into it at his house, not to mention what the matching lingerie he knew was waiting for him under it did to his libido. So he pulled her up and spun her around. A quick tug of her thong to the side and he plunged deep.

He didn't remember saying those words even though he'd more than meant them. But he only meant them for Brynn, damn it.

What a fucking mess.

He stood in the corner of the veranda and sipped on a tonic with lime as she sauntered around the edge of the pool chatting up a few members of the crew and some of the other actors. His entire body felt on edge—restless—and he could barely resist letting a few of the sexier ideas on how he could make this right play out in his mind. She looked like a million bucks in that dress, and those shoes...*dayam*. He'd always loved her in his bed wearing a pair of slinky heels like that.

If he didn't touch her again soon, if she kept dismissing him... A tingle of ire ran up his spine at the thought.

The rhythmic bass of the hip-hop music the DJ spun made the throng of people on the makeshift dance floor grind and pulse against each other. His dick hardened in his jeans at the sight of Brynn standing at the edge wriggling that tight ass of hers to the beat, looking like she'd give anything to be out there in the middle of the crowd.

His heart stopped for a second. Oh, hell *yeah*.

Just as he took a step out of the shadows to head her way, one of the beefy stunt doubles slid up next to her, all suave and cocky in his self-assuredness. She smiled when he whispered in her ear and Ryan had to stomp down the urge to shoot the asshole where he stood.

The guy held out his hand, and Ryan held his breath. Oh, she better not, she *so* better not.

Damn it!

She latched on to no-neck's hand and followed him, gyrating a little as she did so, into the writhing swarm of dancers.

No *way* could he let this happen. The thought of her in another man's arms, of another man touching what was *his*, had him seeing blood red. He set his drink on a table nearby and bulldozed his way through the other party-goers to reach the dance floor. He shoved past flailing arms and ignored intentional gropes until he finally reached her. With a seductive sway of her hips, she spun to face him, her back now to the front of this soon-to-be dead man. But it was when the guy held on to those hips and rubbed against her that Ryan let his inner beast loose.

He grabbed her arm and pulled her to him as he pitched forward and got up in the other guy's face. "Back. The fuck. Off."

The smirk on the ass's lips only pushed Ryan further. His vision darkened and his heart raced. In a flash he had his hand clenched and was a split second away from cocking back to blast the guy when Brynn shouted "No!" and stepped between them.

That was his brave, brave girl. Lord, how he loved this woman.

"Ryan, stop!"

He looked down at her trying to twist her elbow out of his grip. "I'm done playing around," he growled to her. "You're coming with me. Now."

He couldn't give two shits about all the people staring at him as he practically dragged her behind him. His blood was boiling, from the way she pushed him to the edge of reason all the way down to the heat of her skin under his hand.

So much for controlling his rage. She had him on the verge of losing it, teetering that fine line between sanity and monumental stupidity. But this time he knew how to deal with it. Not with hiding behind a drink, or several, but with the God's honest truth.

He came to the last pool cabana at the far end of the veranda and shoved her inside. With a quick yank, he rolled down the canvas flap, tied it closed and turned on her. She stepped back, and Ryan fought even harder to control the raging lust and ferocious love he had for this woman.

There wasn't an ounce of fear in her eyes as she stopped on a dime and held her ground. All he saw was anger and a raw need that only mirrored his own.

"You can't do this," she seethed.

"Too late. I already did."

"I don't want you anymore, Ryan."

"Liar."

Her eyes flared, and he knew right then he'd nailed the truth on the head.

"You want me, and it kills you how much." He crept toward her. "And I've always wanted you. Since the day I first laid eyes on you, I've wanted you."

"Now who's the liar? If you really had…" The rest of the sentence trailed off as she looked away.

Oh he had, all right. He was just too much of an idiot to see what his drinking was doing to them, what it was doing to her. It had been all in good fun, right? Just a couple drinks a day to let loose and enjoy life.

Christ, he never meant for it to get so far out of control.

He lifted her chin with his thumb for her to look at him, but she stepped back, crossed her arms and cocked her head with a vicious glare. He knew the look was supposed to come across as hate-filled and cutting, but with her head tilted like that… Damn, he loved the long angle of her neck and loved even more that tiny spot where her heart pulsed in an erratic rhythm under the skin.

"You're going to listen to me, Brynn," he said, ignoring her sneer as every bit of his body hardened for her.

"Like hell I am."

She dropped her arms and lurched to move past him, but he caught her around the waist before she had the chance to take more than two steps. He wasn't gentle, was beyond thinking rationally as he grasped her wrists in a tight hold and spun her around. He pushed her backwards, step by agonizingly slow step, until he had her pinned against the large pillar in the center of the cabana. He hauled her arms above her head and held them there while he shoved a knee between her thighs.

"Like hell nothing, baby. Enough is enough. We're on my terms now. I'm not letting you run away again."

He lifted his leg, just a little, and rubbed against her. The quick inhale and clench of her jaw told him he wasn't wrong. Everything from this point forward was completely unscripted for them, and now that he had her back in his hold, he'd be damned if he was going to let her walk away without knowing the truth.

"You bastard."

"Not anymore. Maybe I was once, but not anymore, Brynn."

She pushed against him with her hips, still trying to get away, but he held her firm.

"I'll say it again. I'll say it a hundred times if that's what you want. I'm sorry. I'm so fucking sorry."

His kiss couldn't wait, not another second. With a scarcely tamed ferocity, he looked in her eyes and claimed what was his.

She stilled, like the shock of his lips froze her in place before the heat of them coming together melted the ice. She moaned into his mouth and started to kiss him back, only to rip her mouth from his and wrench her head to the side.

"Damn you!" She flashed a look back up at him, her eyes bright with rage in the dim glow of the candles situated around the inside of the cabana. She wriggled against him a bit more. "Let me go!"

"Not until you hear what I have to say." He switched his grip, clasping her wrists within one hand above her head as he brought the other between them. He palmed her flat stomach and stroked along the thin lace of her dress, from her rib cage up and over her breast. The hard bud of her nipple slid between the crevice of his fore and middle fingers and he tightened on it, loving the way she mewled low in her throat when he did. "Not until you let me show you what you mean to me."

Too far gone to even think about stopping, he skimmed his hand higher, to behind her neck, and flicked the clasp of her halter. She closed her eyes and sucked her lips between her teeth as the triangles of material slipped away.

Heaven above, those were pretty. He traced a bare nipple with the tip of his finger and his cock jerked inside his pants. "Look how tight, how red these get for me. Just looking at them has my mouth watering, baby." He nipped at the edge of her jaw. "What I wouldn't give to roll my tongue around one. God, what I wouldn't give to hear you moan as I did it."

Her chest was heaving now, and the sight of her coming undone had him roaring inside and thickening in his jeans even more. He was sure his balls were blue, but he'd hold it in until he could have her, until she begged him to take her.

He continued his torture, slicking kisses over her collarbone and down her chest. "Will you fight me more if I try? Or are you ready to give in to what you need?"

She didn't say a word, but she didn't have to. He felt her desire, savored every nuance of her coming apart under his provocative words, just like she had so many times before.

Shit.

Guilt stabbed him through the heart. He'd missed out on so much with her, so many chances to prove his love, to make her his.

"It's like stepping back in time, back to when we couldn't get enough of each other," he said. "Back to before I fucked it all up."

"Please… Don't," she whispered.

"Please don't what? Admit the truth? Or do this?"

She arched her back as he took her nipple in his mouth and sucked. Gently at first, then harder as she ground against his thigh. He pulled her dress from between her pussy and his leg, fisted and held the bunched material at her waist, and lifted his knee again. She was so hot, so unbelievably hot. Her wetness soaked into his jeans and he had a hell of a time holding back a groan of his own.

He took a chance and released her wrists. He wanted to touch her there, wanted the heat of her juices to coat his fingers. He moved to her other nipple, loving on that one as much as he had the first as he ran his index finger along the thin strap at her hip. When he came to the tiny scrap covering her mound, he couldn't hold back his groan any longer. He dipped his finger inside, and nearly blew apart.

She was completely bare. Holy hell.

"Brynn," he said, swallowing hard and meeting her lust-dazed eyes. "You've been a bad, bad girl. Haven't you?"

Bad didn't even begin to cover it.

He dropped to his knees before she had the chance to say anything. "I have to see this."

To her own surprise, she stood there for him with her arms still above her head, only now she gripped the beveled edges of the pillar so hard she thought her fingers might break.

The dress was still fisted in his hand, and he yanked it, along with that ridiculous barely there thong, down to her ankles.

"Step out," he ordered.

What the fuck was she doing?

But she knew, God she knew to her soul what she was doing as she kicked the dress away and stood again with her legs spread a little wider.

Just as he said he never stopped wanting her, the same was true for her about him. She'd missed this, had wanted him to come to her like this for far too long. Ryan was hers, only hers, and she'd made her mind up right then and there to clutch to the idea he had it in him to change and vowed to hear him out. He meant too much for her to give up on him, too much for her to let him go without a fight.

But she wasn't so ready to let him know all that. Besides, the devil inside her couldn't help but want this first. Him kissing her, stroking her, licking her—her letting him do whatever he wanted, giving him this chance to prove his love and at the same time taking for herself a little of what she'd so desperately missed.

As he knelt at her feet and stared between her legs, she thought she might die. He licked his lips and glanced up at her with that earlier jealousy once again flaring in his eyes. "Who'd you do this for?"

She wasn't going to lie or placate. She'd shaved herself bare that evening in the shower for herself, for the power it gave her, for the sexy way it made her feel, even if at the time she figured no one else would know about it. It was going to be her little secret, her private treat.

"I'm sure you think I did it for you, right?" She let out a little chuckle. "Not hardly. I did it for the one person in my life I can count on. I did it for myself."

He cringed a bit and blew out a harsh breath. "Fuck me," he murmured.

In a heartbeat, she thought.

He lifted a finger and traced along her pussy lips, so slowly, damn it, too slowly, as his other hand slid up her calf and hooked under her knee. He shifted closer to drape her leg over his shoulder and his breath blew in heated waves across her freshly bared skin. She shivered, and when he parted her with two fingers and leaned in for a lick, her knee buckled and she nearly collapsed.

He held her up with his free hand cupping her ass and continued to hold her pussy open with the other. She looked down at him kneeling there between her legs. His eyes were closed as he licked, kissed and loved her with his mouth. She'd never seen him so intent.

She'd never felt anything so amazing.

Her clit pulsed under his tongue and she had to bite her lip to keep from begging. Each lick, every little suck drove her higher. She was spiraling, flying, practically glowing from the heat he created inside her. She needed more, had to have... Dear God, she had to have *more*.

Her hips bucked on their own and she went with it, grinding harder against his tongue. He growled a little and the vibration sent tingles through her clit and into the aching hollow of her pussy.

"God, Ryan," she hissed.

As if he sensed what her words really meant, he moved the hand on her ass closer to her core. So close, so damn close, but not close enough.

"*God,*" she groaned again.

He looked up at her, all clear-eyed, lucid and delicious, and shifted her knee higher on his shoulder. He teased her with his fingers, delving them into the crevice of her ass and sliding them lower, little by torturously little. The tip of his pinkie found its mark, and when she moaned, he swirled it around that tight entrance, pushing gently as the fingers that held her open plunged in one swift motion deep inside her waiting cunt.

She cried out and arched her back at the triple assault. All the air left her lungs when his pinkie breached her anus. At the same instant, he pressed firmly with the fingers of his other hand against her G-spot while his tongue wreaked havoc on her clit. Nearly incoherent from the pleasure—or maybe it was from lack of oxygen or the fact she was once again under the control of the man she never stopped loving—she found it impossible to remain standing and had to grasp the pillar tighter. But he never let up. Deeper his pinkie went, harder and harder he rubbed over that sensitive area inside her.

"Now. Do it now, Brynn. Come for me."

She needed to, badly, and the sultry tone of his words just about had her there. There was something heady in the knowledge that he alone held the power of her pleasure in his hands, in his mouth. With another low growl, he pursed his lips and drew on her clit with quick, feverish sucks. The scattered tingles in her belly tightened and centered, cramped almost with a strong ache to release, and when he gave one final suck and one last deep push of his fingers, she let every bit of that pleasure claim her.

She muffled the moans, cries and pants of her orgasm by pressing her mouth against her raised arm and squeezing her eyes shut as he drew out every last tremor. He kissed the inside of her thigh as his fingers left her and before she knew what he was doing, he'd lifted her in his arms and carried her to a heap of pillows in the corner of the cabana. After he carefully set her down, he knelt beside her and started unbuttoning his shirt.

"This is the real me, Brynn. The man who hurt you, the asshole I was, died that night six months ago. I need for you to know that I won't ever go back to that place. I swear I'll never disappoint you again."

She'd dreamed time and again of him saying that to her. And now that he had, his sincerity compelled her to listen to the rest.

"I need only one thing from you before we go any further."

He ripped the shirt from his body and leaned over her to cup her cheek. "Anything, baby. God, I'll give you anything."

"Then give me the truth." She held on to his wrist and whispered, "I need to know why, Ryan. Just please, tell me *why*."

Chapter Six

Ah hell, that's what Ryan had spent months in rehab trying to figure out. He didn't have those typical reasons like child abuse, money troubles or low self-esteem. If anything, he'd been *too* cocky. Not that he had a God complex, but there for a while he thought nothing could touch him or that he could do no wrong.

Pretty far off the mat with that idea.

He swirled his thumbs on her cheeks and tenderly kissed her swollen lips. This was it. This was the chance he'd been waiting months for. His blood was still rushing through his veins and his cock felt like it might explode, but as he lay next to her and propped himself up on one elbow so he could talk to her face to face, he pushed all that out of his mind.

He trailed his fingers from her cheek, down between her breasts and over her stomach. "I wish I had some sort of miracle answer for you, but the truth is, I don't." He glanced from his hand dancing around her belly button up to her face. "I fucked up."

"That's it? All I get is *I fucked up*?" She let out a weary sigh. "God, Ryan."

He threw his leg over hers when she started to squirm. "Stop. Just stop and listen, okay?"

For a minute he thought she might refuse him like she had earlier. But to his relief, she settled back beside him and quieted down. She blew strands of sweaty bangs off her forehead, lifted an arm above her head and swallowed a bit harder than normal.

"I've imagined so many scenarios of you telling me why you did what you did," she said. "I have to admit, though, most of them ended with you either bloody or unconscious."

He nodded and could tell from the look in her eyes she was more than serious. "I don't deserve anything less."

The tense set of her muscles relaxed a fraction at that. "I've been cheated on before, Ryan. I'm not naïve. It happens all the time, especially in this business. But the way we were together, how it all felt… I just never expected it. Not from you."

The pain stabbing through his heart couldn't be anywhere close to the pain she'd gone through. The pain he'd put her through. "You're right, you know. I can say I'm sorry and admit to how much I fucked up until I'm blue in the face, but in the end I know none of that will matter, not until I've earned back your trust." He edged a little closer, wanting so badly to take her, to have one more chance to feel her tighten around him. But beyond all that, he'd really love nothing more than to have another opportunity to just kiss her again. God, he could still taste her heavenly juices on his lips, on his tongue.

"I don't know any other way to say it. I did fuck up. You'll never know how many times I wanted to die knowing I put you through all that."

"What happened?"

He dropped his head to her shoulder and spoke softly against her skin. "I lost control."

"You lost control?"

"God, I know how lame that sounds. And believe me, it took long enough for me to build up to admitting it. Even now it's difficult to say."

She twisted in his arms to face him. "Go on."

"Did you know our first meeting wasn't an accident?"

Her eyebrows drew together and she looked at him like he had four heads. "What's that got to do with—"

"Just hear me out," he interrupted. "I'd gotten wind you were going to be at that fundraiser. I canceled an out of town photo shoot and really pissed off my manager just so I could go." He laughed a little and stroked lightly down her waist and over her hip. "I even got there an hour early to make sure I wouldn't miss you walking in."

"But why?"

Now he was the one looking at her like she'd sprouted a new noggin. "You know why. You felt it, same as I did. I know you did. And when I introduced myself and you slipped your hand in mine, I not only felt it, but I *saw* it. I saw that fire in your eyes."

She looked lower, at his throat, but didn't say anything so he went on. "I knew we'd hit it off, but I had no idea how lost I'd get in you."

Her gaze flew up and she pierced him with a stare. "You're blaming this on me?"

Oh, fuck, that wasn't what he meant. "Shit, no. Not at all." He flopped to his back and stared at the ceiling. "All I meant is that I could be the real me when I was with you. It all felt so… I don't know. Natural. Real. There wasn't any of that Hollywood bullshit between us."

"So, why then?" she asked, cuddling up beside him and propping her chin on his chest. "Why the drinking? Why the…"

Hell, she couldn't even say it. Why the cheating? His gut wrenched a little more.

It was her turn to swirl her fingers over his skin, and as she traced the muscle lines along his stomach, he lifted his hand next to hers and held it open for her to take. She hesitated, but only for a second before sliding her fingers over his palm just like she'd done that first night he met her. He grasped them tightly, afraid that if he let go he might lose his nerve. They lay together quietly like that, hand in hand, until he'd formed in his head what he really wanted to say.

"I've always hated excuses, the way people make up stupid-assed reasons or lay the responsibility on someone else for the things they do. I won't pull that with you. All I have to offer is the truth." He met her gaze, and the hope there gave him the fortitude to keep going. "But before I get into the nitty-gritty, I need to tell you about that night at the premiere."

He rolled to his side and she rested her head on his biceps. Her hand was still within his as he brought it to his chest and pressed her palm over his heart.

"Brynn, I believed it was you in that coat closet with me. I know it's no explanation, and I hate saying it, but I was so wasted that night. Beyond wasted. Me and the guys had been doing shots since the after-party started, and when I headed for the bathroom… It was like this weird slow-motion, fast-forward thing. Everything happened so fast, but so slowly too. I'd been dying to get my hands on you all night. I'd spent most of the premiere not watching the movie, but looking at you through the corner of my eye and imagining how that dress would look fisted in my hand and bunched around your waist."

She closed her eyes and pressed her cheek into his arm.

"And then I looked up and saw you. I wanted to die. Part of me actually did. The bad part. The drunk part."

When she looked at him again, her eyes glistened with a sheen of tears. One fell and ran in a stream down his arm. The warmth of that one drop, the tiniest confirmation of all the hurt he caused her, had him fighting back a mortified cry.

"People say they know when they've hit rock bottom." He pressed her hand harder on his chest and he wanted to groan when she flexed her fingertips against his skin. "That night, the devastation I caused both of us, Brynn, that was my rock bottom."

Their gazes met once again and she whispered, "Oh, Ryan."

Jesus, he wanted so badly to kiss her, to kiss away all the hurt still in her eyes. But he had to hold back until he told her the rest.

"I can only imagine what you thought when I didn't call you afterwards, the shit that ran through your mind when I didn't show up at your place. I bet you expected me to break down your door and pass it off as no big deal."

One shoulder lifted. "I figured you didn't want me, that what we had was over."

That earlier sick roil hit his stomach again full-force. "Oh baby, nothing could be further from the truth. I wanted you so much. But I knew, even in my delirium I felt to my bones that I would only get worse. As I watched that cab drive away with you inside and realized what I'd done… Well, there was only one thing that I *could* do."

"Rehab?" she asked.

"Three solid months' worth."

"You went that night?"

He played with a lock of her hair while still holding her hand over his heart. "Yeah, I never even went home. I called my manager from the hotel. Honestly, I think he was relieved. He set it all up and had the driver take me straight there. It was the best decision, if not the hardest one, that I ever made."

She tucked her head under his chin and rubbed her lips over his chest. He held her tighter, dying to feel her mouth not only there, but everywhere on his body, all at once.

"And what did you walk away with?"

He sighed. "That I am my father's son."

She peered up at him with a quizzical look. "I don't follow."

He cupped her cheek and pressed his forehead against hers. "My father was a drunk, Brynn. He left when I was young, so I never spent too much time around him. But the stories I'd overhear, not just from my mom, but from a slew of other family members as well… Let's just say he had some major issues."

"Ryan, I'm so sorry."

He shook his head. "No blaming, remember? But at the same time, I never knew how big a part genetics played. Alcoholism runs in my dad's family and I guess he passed the tendency on to me."

"So that's why…"

He squeezed his eyes for a moment and fought back a renewed wave of regret. "Partially. That and an over-inflated ego. I was just an ass, Brynn. An ass with lack-of-control issues. One drink never led to a second, it led to ten. I was so caught up in my own supposed *greatness* that I couldn't see the forest for the trees. My addictive personality took center stage." He huffed out a breath. "Hell, more like took over my life. I let it all get too far out of control."

"And now?" she asked, caressing his cheek, too.

"Now?" He couldn't hold back a little smile. "I'm good, Brynn. I've never been so clear. I understand my past and strive every day not to repeat the shitty things I've done. Some days are easier than others, and I know it'll always be like that. But today, it's a good day. Being with you, holding you and touching you like this, makes it absolutely perfect."

"I never wanted to admit how much I missed you, but God, I did."

"Ah, baby. I won't ever put you through that again. My heart is yours, only yours. Please tell me you can find a way to forgive me."

Her eyes searched his as she bit her lower lip and smiled. "Oh Ryan, I already have."

That one look, combined with the words he'd waited months to hear, floored him, possessed him. He growled low in his chest and came over her as every cell in his body sparked to life with a primal need. She lay on her back, and as he covered her body with his, she slid her hands between them and reached for the button on his jeans.

"We start over, right here, right now, with this. A promise to each other to always be open, to always be honest. No more hiding, no more looking the other way," she said. "And no more being apart."

"Never again," he groaned as she lowered his zipper. When she reached her hand inside his pants and gripped his cock, he shuddered. She smiled again, and he couldn't get over the sexy tilt to her lips, the blatant need in her eyes.

He knelt between her spread legs and barely got his jeans past his hips before she pulled him back over her again. He wanted inside her so badly, and he could tell by the way she drew up her knees, arched her back and latched on to his neck with a ferocious grip that she was dying for him every bit as much as he was dying for her.

Balanced on his elbows above her, he held her gaze and slipped inside her. Oh God, she felt so good. So welcoming. So tight. So fucking amazing. Slowly he moved, inch by inch, allowing her to adjust to his width and drawing out not only her pleasure, but his own as well.

Her eyes drifted closed and she inclined her neck, inviting him in. He licked over the hollow before moving to the side and nipping along the sensitive flesh there. She forked her fingers through his hair and held him closer.

He could hardly breathe, could barely keep up the torture of his slow thrusts. He wanted to drive into her, over and over, faster and faster until they lost themselves in the passion, in the power flaring between them.

A little harder, heaven help him, a little quicker now. She moved with him, against him, met him push for pull. He slammed his lips against hers and cupped her breast. She groaned into his mouth only to break away to hiss out a breath when he rolled her nipple between his thumb and forefinger.

"Oh God," she cried.

"Baby, I…I…" He wanted to say it, to tell her he loved her, but wasn't so sure he should. Not like this, with the memories of that night in the coat closet so fresh. He'd be damned if he'd hurt her like that again, so he bit back what he really wanted to say and dove for her breast instead.

"It's okay," she said, lifting his head away from her chest. "I want you to say it. I need you to. It's just you and me this time. No one else. Please, I need to hear the words from your lips. I need to hear them as you look into my eyes."

Nothing could stop him from telling her then, not a solitary thing. The love he held inside tumbled from his mouth, from his heart. "I love you, Brynn. I have since I first saw you. I don't want you to ever doubt that. Never doubt my love for you."

She practically beamed under him. "I don't, not anymore."

"Thank God," he whispered and kissed her harder as he drove himself fully into her.

She bit at his lips, mewling, panting, and he knew this—being in her arms, in her life—was where he was meant to be. Fate, the once cold and unfeeling bitch, had softened and come around for him full circle. Nothing but a bountiful destiny awaited them. And as she tightened and pulsed along his length, then pulled from his mouth to cry out as she came, his soul, for the first time he ever remembered, felt mended. Felt whole.

With a guttural groan, he came with her, spilling his seed inside her and marking her as his. She drew every drop from his body, and as they lay together in the breathless, sweaty aftermath of their lovemaking, he met her gaze once again. Satisfaction, pride and desire welled in his chest at the passion he saw there. A passion for life, a passion for him. He loved this woman with every part of his being, from the top of her head, all the way down to her more-than-suckable, pink bubble-gum toes.

CHASING EDEN

Dedication

To my "bestest" friend Mary and to "Pop Rocks" Penny. You've blessed me with your friendship, your encouragement and, as my beta readers, you kept me on task by asking repeatedly when I was going to get the next chapters to you. It means so much to me to know you loved this story and you couldn't wait to read more of Shane and Eden's journey.

Trademarks Acknowledgement

The author acknowledges the trademarked status and trademark owners of the following wordmarks mentioned in this work of fiction:

Tiger Beat Magazine: Laufer Media, Inc.

Chapter One

Eden Foster stared between the licks of flames shooting four feet above the bonfire, still unable to believe rock-star bad-boy Shane Tolan, lead singer and sinful front man of the smoldering-hot band Blackguard, sat on the other side. Propped against a huge old oak tree, he lounged on a blanket, casual and relaxed as can be. Long, lean legs were crossed at his ankles, powerful arms over his chest.

Mercy, mercy. What she wouldn't give to press her lips against the lower portion of that sexy Celtic lion tattoo showing just past the rolled up sleeve of his left arm, or to trace her tongue along the thick black stroke of the tat's tail where it morphed into a tangle of classic Celtic knots below his elbow.

Okay… A serious diversion right about now would be a good thing. A great thing. A *necessary* thing. But Eden knew getting any sort of distraction with Shane in such close proximity would be next to impossible.

She certainly wasn't a stranger to the idiosyncratic world of celebrity, so she could hardly blame being all googly-eyed star-struck as the reason for her sudden inability to breathe. As a highly recognized graphic artist to some of the fastest rising names in the music business, she'd lost track of how many times she'd met and mingled with hotter-than-hot Top Ten performers. But none of them—not a single, solitary one—compared to Shane Tolan.

All six-foot-two sweltering paradise of him.

God, she wanted to *kill* little Mrs. Ava Banford for not telling her he'd be here. Did her best friend not know her at all? How could something like his attendance not be the first thing Ava blurted out as soon as Eden walked through her friend's front door tonight, never mind the courtesy of a quick phone call hours ahead of time? And what about the fact that Eden had been trying for more than six months to get Gregory Banford to set up a pitch meeting with Shane and his band? As Ava's husband and producer of Blackguard's latest CD, Gregory had all the clout she needed to pull the meeting off, but the timing never seemed to work out quite right for any of them.

And now here she was, practically face to face with the one man who could send her mind and libido in a thousand different directions all at once, completely and utterly unprepared.

Oh no, killing Ava would be too good for her. Torture… Yeah, a little torture might make Eden feel a hell of a lot better right now. Lord, she hated to be caught off guard like this.

In the midst of planning Ava's demise over her surprise ambush, Eden also didn't want to think about how her entire body reacted to Shane's presence like some sort of hormonal teenager, all tingly and magnetic. Normally she'd never let a good-looking—yeah right, understatement of the century right there—*gorgeous* man get the better of her, but this particular rock star had the uncanny ability to knock the breath right out of her lungs with nothing more than a lascivious look.

Earlier, after their quick introduction, he'd lifted her hand to his lips in the most sensual handshake she'd ever experienced. Since then he'd peered at her a few times throughout the night with devilish grins and the sexiest eyes this side of sane. And now, three hours into Ava's thirty-fifth birthday party-slash-bonfire, she found herself across from the object of all her fantasies, stealing furtive glances through stupid orange flames.

Ava leaned closer and whispered in her ear. "Stop ogling. Geez, show at least a hint of self-restraint."

She suddenly hated Ava as much as one person could possibly hate another but, God help her, she loved the little witch just as much, too. "Bite me, Av." No, wait, on second thought... "You should know better than anyone how I hate to be blindsided like this. A heads-up would've been appreciated."

Ava snickered. "And that's *exactly* why I didn't say anything. I know how long you've been dying to win Blackguard as a client. You'd have waltzed in here tonight in full-out business mode instead of party mode. But nuh-uh. Not tonight, Ede. It's my *birshhday...*"

Okay, seems Ava had enjoyed one too many Cosmos.

She giggled again. "You need to relax. We're supposed to be having fun here. Celebrating."

Oh yeah, Eden would celebrate all right, as soon as she landed Shane's band and the contract to design their new CD cover. Industry grapevines being what they were, she knew the band was on the prowl for a new, edgier concept, and Eden was more than determined to provide that very thing. The perfect images haunted her mind. Deep hues, striking poses. God, she could do so much for him...

She could do even more *to* him.

Stop it, Eden! Think CD covers here, not body covers.

But her mind wouldn't listen. As much as she'd love to sign his band, she still couldn't resist the man himself. Every dream she'd had for the last year starred Shane, every secret fantasy had his mouth sucking that perfect spot on her neck, his hands stroking her skin, his cock stroking elsewhere.

Would this really be his business you're wanting, Eden? Or more likely your pleasure?

Frustrated with all the ill-timed erotic ideas filling her head, she rubbed her forehead and casually stole another quick peek. Shane was laughing with the guy next to him. A record mixer, if memory served. With a swipe of his hand through his luscious tobacco-colored mane, he cocked his head and settled his gaze on her. A lift at the edge of Shane's lips and a gleam in his eyes—a glimmer that *had* to be a trick of the firelight—made her heart stutter wildly, which was just so pathetically bodice-ripping-sappy-romance-novel cliché she wanted to laugh. Instead, she sucked in a breath and turned away.

"You've completely sideswiped me here, Av. I can't even think straight."

With one brow lifted over her shocking blue eyes, Ava grinned and tapped a perfectly French-manicured fingernail on her Cosmo glass. "Seems so. But, just *why* is that?"

Oh crap. Eden knew that look. Lord help them all when Ava began pondering life's little mysteries.

The fire crackled and popped as sparks danced above it before they flitted into nothingness in the air. Gregory and Ava's summer home was the perfect hideaway to hold the weekend birthday bash. But with Eden's sudden inability to focus on anything other than the man on the other side of the fire, she wished the party had been held in the city. On her own turf, where she'd be the one in charge.

Unable to resist, she snuck another glance back to Shane and worked her lower lip between her teeth before releasing it on a sigh. Ava's grin blossomed into a triumphant smirk.

"Ah-ha! So *that's* it. Here I am thinking you're about to go all business executive on me, when the reality is that you, Miss-Always-In-Control, have the hots for a wild rocker." She chuckled again, then lifted her glass to her lips as her gaze slid from Eden to Shane. "Got to be honest with you here, Ede, that's really not what I expected from you," she said after a sip. "At least not if we go by the last, say, half-dozen guys you've dated. Have we finally found a weakness in that tough-as-nails, control-freak exterior you're so famous for?"

Eden feigned nonchalance with a lazy shrug. A pathetic show, really, and she knew right then she'd given herself away. She smiled with a grin of her own. "Busted. So I have a thing for rock guys. Sue me."

"Well, well. Wonders never cease," Ava mused on a wicked smile.

Eden's smile, however, faded and she threw her friend an exasperated look. "He's *so* not my type, Av. You know me, I'm business twenty-four-seven. Building up Imagining Eden is usually all I think about. But every time I look at Shane or hear one of his songs, let alone that velvet voice of his, everything flies right out the window and all I can think about is getting my hands on him." She sighed and fiddled with the wine charm on her own glass. "Hell, listen to me. I sound like a little girl ogling an issue of *Tiger Beat*."

"No you don't. Besides, I think this is perfect." Ava tipped back the last of the sweet, pink cocktail. "Still Ede, no matter if he's your type or not, you never back down from looks as hot as he's giving you. He's coming just short of eating you up with those sexy eyes of his and you're the queen of giving as good as you get. So really, what's the matter?"

Yeah, Eden? What's the matter?

She could try to convince herself the rest of tonight and most of tomorrow she was only interested in Shane in a purely business way, but deep down she knew it'd do no good. A contract with his band sure as hell would be nice, but more than that, she wanted the rock star. The bad boy.

The man.

Ava leaned closer, persistent as a playful puppy and thankfully just as loyal. "He's gorgeous, his band has the number two song in the country, a song that's expected to be number one by next week." Her voice softened as she reached out and laid her hand on Eden's arm. "But more importantly, sweetie, he also happens to be one of the nicest guys I've ever met. I say go for it. And I'm talking the man, Ede. Not the job."

Go for it…

Should she? Could she let go, give in to her secret temptation and, for once, put her wants and desires before the responsibility of growing her company?

Behind them, the sliding glass door to the four-thousand-square-foot lakeside villa opened on a whoosh. With an outrageous flaming cake held precariously in his hands, Gregory navigated his way down the stairs from the deck toward the fire pit. Once he started singing, the other twenty or so guests chimed right in along with him.

"Happy birthday to you..."

The rest of the song fell halfheartedly from her lips as she stole another glimpse across the glittery fire. Shane sang along too, but his eyes... Oh hell, he was staring right at her again. He smiled on the last note, and she thought for sure she'd die when his tongue peeked out to lick along his lower lip.

Good Lord, the man was sex on a stick.

Harder to do this time, but while Ava stood to blow out her birthday candles, Eden averted her gaze. She needed a minute or two away from his stare to gather her wits. Which, of course, was way easier said than done. The rush his looks created had her insides resembling that of a lava lamp. Gooey. Melty.

Downright hot.

Ava puffed out her cheeks to blow out the last candle before kissing Gregory and plopping back onto the blanket. She stuck out her lower lip in a playful, drunken pout. "I'm old, baby. Thirty-five. Over the hill."

The group of close-knit friends chuckled at Ava's ridiculous observation. Gregory handed the cake off to the waitstaff behind him and squatted to peck his wife's nose with a quick kiss. "Never old, sweetheart. You're perfect."

"I need something to make me feel young again," she teased as Greg dropped down next to her on the blanket. "I know!" The high-pitch squeal of the statement nearly broke Eden's eardrums. "This is perfect! Let's play a game, like when I was a kid." She practically glowed as she grabbed Eden's hand. "When I was little all the neighborhood kids would get together after dark to play hide-and-seek. That's it! We're all going to play a good old-fashioned game of hide-and-seek."

Groans and laughter circled the fire pit. Eden even heard a muttered, "Oh, hell no."

But then Shane dropped his hands to his thighs, leaned forward and flashed a grin so hot it put the roaring fire to shame. "This could be fun. I'll even be 'it'."

It?

Hmm… He was more than *it*. He was…

Eden stopped the analogy. She knew damn well what he was.

Raw. Edgy.

To die for.

He rose and sauntered around the outskirts of the fire with such a sexy gait that her mouth went dry just as other parts of her body moistened. Her nipples tightened at the lazy smile that blessed his lips.

"I'm supposed to hide my eyes and count, right?"

Caught in a trance, she jumped when Ava tugged on her hand to pull her to her feet. Shane stood right beside her, and when he stuffed his hands in his back pockets and loomed closer, she got a whiff of his heavenly cologne. Dark and spicy, just like the man.

Oh, boy…

Ava brought her out of another stupor with a squeeze on her fingers. "Yes. Count to at least twenty. No, make that fifty." She grinned at Gregory with an evil smile. "Come on, hide with me, baby."

The pair took off like a shot. Eden had a good feeling they had no intention of participating in the game Ava herself had suggested.

The rest of the guests ignored them as they ran off. They settled back around the bonfire and laughed about how their hosts still acted like teenagers even after years of marriage.

"If you ask me," Blackguard's lead guitarist, Brett O'Neal, said as he lifted his prized Brazilian Redwood acoustic from its case nearby and strummed a hypnotic chord. "An impromptu jam session around the campfire sounds better than running around in the dark like a fool anyway."

Shane turned back to Eden. His eyes blazed, and this time it wasn't from a trick of the firelight. "I'm not so sure about that," he whispered, low enough that only she heard him. "Playing in the dark sounds like it might be right up my alley. You still game?"

Her breath caught somewhere inside her chest, as did any words she might've thought to say. "Game?" she finally murmured.

He stepped closer, his eyes dark and sensual. Sultry heat encompassed her and his diabolic grin proved disastrous against her control. "Yeah, game. You know, as in have a little fun?"

Her body flooded with a swift rush of heat. The business persona she relied so heavily upon vanished at those simple words, and in its place emerged the woman she desperately wanted him to consume in a thousand different ways.

"You don't remember me, do you?"

"What?" she asked, her mind instantly torn between his magnetic warmth and sudden confusion.

With a gentle hand, he lifted her chin and studied her eyes. "God, it really is you. I wasn't so sure at first."

"What are you talking about?"

"Look at me, Eden. Remember me?"

She looked, but the only recognition that flared was an image of him from his latest music video, guitar strapped across his back with a death grip on the microphone stand, sexy and desirable as sin. The mental picture was enough to make her want to strike a deal with the devil himself for just an hour alone with him and his scrumptious body.

"Think back about eight years, at a weekend beach party for some studio executive's daughter. My old band was one of about five that played that weekend. You were there."

"I was..." Eight years ago—her senior year at USC. She closed her eyes as memories from that weekend so long ago returned, as did the painful recollection of the hangover she'd ended up with afterward. She could still feel the throb along her eyebrows as she opened her eyes again. "Simone Holloway's graduation party."

When he edged closer, she stepped back.

"Yeah, Simone. That was her name." He continued forward, seductively stalking her, his tight-muscled chest only inches away from her now-aching nipples as she moved backward with him. "You gave me the hottest kiss I'd ever had in my life that weekend."

She stopped in her tracks. "I did *what*?"

He bumped into her and laughed. Even something as simple as a steadying hand coming around her lower back made her skin tingle and vibrate. God, his touch was so damn *electric*.

"I knew you'd had a few that night, but I have to say I'm crushed you don't remember me. *Or* that kiss..."

As he pushed a stray strand of hair over her shoulder, she struggled to ignore her reactions to his heat. Instead she tried her best to concentrate on the events of that long-ago grad party. The festivities had started early on a Saturday morning and continued on until late Sunday night. Simone's father had spared no expense. What his little girl wanted, his little girl got, usually with no questions asked. And with that knowledge—and they all knew despite her father's wishes—Simone had made sure there was enough liquid libation for everyone who attended.

Yeah, Eden had been seriously buzzed that first night. But even so, she certainly hadn't drunk enough to not remember. Had she?

Her heart rate picked up double-time while her breathing became shallower. She studied Shane's face as best she could in the dim glow away from the fire. He appeared…well, somewhat different from the recent haunting images on her small television screen or those touched-up photos in the rock magazines. The strong jaw, the powerful angle of his nose, those luscious lips—and the way they tilted at the corners—each distinct feature played at the edge of her mind.

The bad-boy rocker…

Oh God. He…he couldn't be. Could he?

But even as she asked herself, she knew the answer.

"Your band went on late, right? After midnight." Her breasts swelled and her mind whirled with the memory. Flutters bunched together in her stomach. "You…you had me hooked from the second you stepped up to the microphone. I couldn't stop staring at you while you were singing. You jumped off stage about an hour later. Sweaty, sticky, but that didn't matter to me." More tingles coursed through her body, fire lanced between her thighs.

"You came from behind and touched my arm," he added.

Yeah, she had. She'd wanted to touch his tattoo, a seductively designed Celtic Tree of Life high on his right biceps. Mystified, she tried to swallow, but her throat remained bone dry. "You turned around…"

"And then you kissed me. Not a word from you. Just hot, wicked lips." He smiled. "And plenty of tongue."

It took enormous effort to not stand there and gape at him. How could she not have connected the drop-dead gorgeous man he was now with that hot, young rocker from years ago? God, no wonder she was so drawn to him. She could arguably say that her somewhat fuzzy recollection of the skinny, long-haired singer had spurred her secret obsession for hard-driving, hard-rocking musicians.

It was him.

Scents and sounds instantly amplified. Thrust back in time, she actually felt the stickiness of her skin that hot, humid night. Smelled the citronella from the tiki lamps that mingled with the salty breeze of the ocean beyond the beach. Relived the tingle of his lips, soft and warm against hers.

"You tasted like…a little like mint."

He cupped her cheek and brushed his thumb over her lower lip. "Yeah? Well, you tasted like beer."

She chuckled and spun away, breathless. Amazed. "I bet I did."

After a few steps, she peered over her shoulder. It was all she could do to keep the tentative hold on her wavering control. The last thing she wanted was to come off like some sort of teeny-bopper-crazed fan. Nor was she that impetuous young woman anymore. No, now she was a professional—smart, respected…

And damn it, *so* far out of her league.

"You've changed. Your hair's shorter. And… Well, you're a little bigger now."

He followed her and smirked. "Yeah. I ditched the grunge look, cleaned up some and joined a gym. I met Brett a few years ago and we hooked up with a couple other awesome musicians. The rest, as they say, is rock and roll history."

"You make it sound so easy."

He huffed. "No, definitely not easy. The glamorous rock-star life is more than just a myth."

They'd worked themselves halfway past the gentle sloped edge beyond the fire pit. Down the hill lay the warm lake she'd swum in so often on long weekends here. But further up on the opposite rise sat the small guest cottage where she always stayed whenever she visited.

"Where'd you go after that night, Eden? You laid one hell of a kiss on me and then your friends dragged you away. You never said a word. I had to ask around for hours just to find out your first name."

Crickets and frogs sang together in the underbrush and trees as she turned to face him. The swish from the gentle waves of the lake below and the glow on the water from the full moon painted such a serene, seductive picture.

Pleasure seeped from every pore of the delicious man in front of her. She couldn't speak, couldn't form even the simplest word. He inched closer until his chest pressed against hers. The zing from his touch stole her breath. He snaked his hands down her arms and wound his fingers between hers. As he lowered his head, he brought her hands to the small of her back and clasped her wrists together within one of his. He tightened his grip and tugged ever so slightly. She winced at the force, but the thrill of his dominance, combined with the hungry way his gaze devoured her, had her more than ready to make all those dreams she'd had about him come true.

"I've been chasing after the thought of you for eight long years. No way are you getting away from me this time, baby."

With his lips a breath away from hers, he reached between their bodies with his free hand, stroked a hard nipple through her thin cotton blouse with the back of his knuckles and licked the seam of her lips with a tongue so hot, she knew he'd burned her for sure.

"So, what do you say, sweet Eden? Wanna play with me now?"

Chapter Two

Two words burst through her mind—*hell* and *yeah*. But she couldn't move them past her lips. Instead, she stared at his mouth, imagined his more-than-full lips consuming hers, or covering a taut nipple. Or licking lower on her body, where she dreamed of having him so many times before.

Her breasts heaved against his abs on every breath. She ached, wanted. Wanted her bad boy. Wanted Shane.

The edge of his lip quirked. "What's the matter? Cat got your tongue?"

The childish cliché brought her out of a stupefied daze. She bit her lip to buy herself a moment, all the while hovering a little too close to the brink of lost control.

"Tell ya what," he crooned as he loosened the grip on her wrists. "I'll even give you a head start. Count, like I'm supposed to. But not to fifty. Not even twenty. Oh no, baby. You get the count of ten. Then I'm coming after you."

His voice, smooth and low with the slightest hint of an Irish brogue she hadn't really noticed before, oozed over her senses like a coating of sticky honey. Desire laced every one of his words.

A short-lived wave of self-confidence replaced her utter amazement as the need for him intensified. "Only ten? I won't get very far."

His day-old beard prickled and scratched along her cheek when he nuzzled against her. A warm, even breath blew over her ear and sent tremors racing down her spine. "That's the idea. I told you, I'm not letting you get away this time."

Her heart pounded, not only in her chest, but in every vein, pore and cell throughout her body. And Christ, he smelled so good. One lick… Please, give her just one lick on that strong, powerful neck he kept just out of reach.

"Then why should I even try?"

A deep chuckle vibrated against her breasts. "Ah, come on, babe. Call it the thrill of the chase. Even if it is a short one." He pulled back, looked down at her with powerful, searing eyes. The stark desire in his gaze floored her. "I saw it in you then and I see it in you now, Eden. The wild child hidden beneath the professional exterior, the naughty woman begging to be released." He slid his hand lower between them until he cupped the hot denim that covered her throbbing core. He stroked her slowly, firmly. "You feel it here. The rush, the ache."

Her eyes drifted shut and her head rolled back to her shoulders. Warm lips nipped her chin, then moved lower along her neck.

All of what he said was true, so true…

How did he know? What gave her away? And could she, *should* she give in to it?

"Ready now?" He stroked harder through the seam of her jeans. God, she could've come right then. "One…"

When she lifted her head to meet his gaze, the fire inside burned even hotter.

"Two…" He gave her another devilish, crooked smile. "You'd better go, Eden. I've waited such a long time. You don't want to keep me waiting much longer, do you? Come on, baby, make me run after you."

He removed his hand and she wanted to scream. *No, no!*

"Go ahead. I'll find you. And once I do, I'm going to blow away the memory of that kiss years ago."

The heat from his seductive eyes compelled her to move. She twisted her wrists from his grip, spun from his arms as some sort of mesmerizing force carried her toward the hill. She knew exactly where to go, exactly where she wanted to lead him.

"Three..."

The word floated on the air right behind her and she turned to flick a peek over her shoulder. He wasn't hiding his eyes to count like a child would. Oh, no. He stood tall, his stance wide. Thick arms hung at his sides, devastating eyes bored into hers.

The sly grin on his lips belied the fire from his stare. And this time when he counted, he stepped toward her. "Four..."

Let the chase begin.

With a sudden playful edge, she laughed—all girlishly giggly, which was just so unlike her—and ran up the hill. She climbed the stairs to the wide terrace of the guest house two at a time and shoved through the front door. Not looking behind her, but feeling his intense presence closing in nonetheless, she raced through the house toward the back, past the gourmet kitchen, around the dining room table and out a set of French double doors that led to a huge balcony.

Breathless from the thrill of the run—or was it more from the knowledge of what was to come?—she lurched into the corner, grabbed the railing and took in the stunning view. Nocturnal life pulsed from the forest beyond and a spectacular harvest moon hung high in the dark sky. From it, a vivid, silvery glow washed over every surface. Its brilliance made seeing easy, despite the late hour.

Eden turned her back to the picturesque scenery and eagerly waited. Waited for Shane to find her, waited for every one of her dreams to be realized.

Thank God she didn't have to wait long.

With a predatory pace, he emerged from the shadows inside the house. Moonlight emphasized his dark European coloring, accentuated every rakish nuance. He stopped and splayed his arms, gripped the jamb on both sides of the double doors with hands so large and powerful, she shivered.

Oh Lord, he was even more magnificent in the flesh than he'd been in her dreams. Black biker boots covered his feet. Dark, loose jeans hung belted from trim, narrow hips and she was surprised to see he'd unbuttoned his shirt somewhere along the chase. Instead of the dryness she experienced before, her mouth now watered when she glimpsed the shadows of an impressive six-pack, the cut of hard-muscled pecs. A tattoo she'd never seen before curved above his left nipple. As he stalked across the deck toward the railing—toward *her*—she made out the single word in beautiful Gaelic script: *Blasdag*. She had no idea what the word meant, and the tattoo only added to his mystery.

Mere inches away, he gripped the railing on either side of her hips and leaned closer. She arched her back and tamped down a new barrage of belly flutters at the sheer determination etched upon his face.

"Five."

When he crashed against her lips, his succulent mouth stole all rational thought and his feverish tongue devoured any sane notion that might've lingered in her befuddled mind. Only their mouths touched, but the effortless way he consumed her was more than enough to drive her insane.

He broke free and she moaned.

"God, that was it, Eden. *That's* what's haunted me for years."

"Shane…"

"More. Give me more." He kissed her again, only this time he gathered her in his arms and roamed his hands over her back. One slid down to cup her ass, the other went higher to tangle in the hair at her nape. Below his belt buckle, his erection pressed firmly against her lower belly as he held her tighter.

She couldn't think, didn't want to. All she craved was right here, right now—Shane in her arms.

He left her lips to lick his way down her neck. "Do you want me?"

What? Was he serious? Did he honestly think she'd be this breathless right now if she didn't?

He stopped the torture of his lips to stare at her. "Tell me you're not just caught up in the moment, Eden. Tell me you want me—the *real* me—as much as I want you." There went that little lift to the edge of his lip again. "I've thought so many times of what I'd like to do to that sweet woman who nearly brought me to my knees years ago with a single kiss. And now that I have you, I can't walk away. God, don't ask me to."

She caressed his rough cheeks and stared into his sultry eyes. "You've lived in my subconscious for years, Shane. Yes, I want you. With a helplessness I really don't understand."

With a loss of control she'd only felt once before in her life, she raised to her toes and kissed him with all the pent-up passion she'd kept hidden inside for ages. Hidden since the last time she let loose and kissed him eight years ago. She sucked his lips, pulled the lower one between her teeth, then let go with a nip. "I don't want you to walk away. Stay. Show me all the naughty things that have been missing in my life."

He groaned and held her tight against his chest. "My little wild child," he whispered against her lips. "I think I just fell in love."

She started to smile, but he stole her reaction with a kiss so forceful her entire body instantly turned to jelly. Pliant within his arms, she melted further as he spun and walked her backward until her calves hit the double-wide chaise lounge in the center of the balcony. He gently lowered them together until she lay with the soft cushion under her and Shane's hard, taut body above.

His hips nestled flawlessly within the juncture of her thighs. The thickness of his cock rubbed against her in perfectly synchronized waves as his pelvis imitated the action of his tongue deep in her mouth. But all she could think about was what else she wanted there. The desperation to feel him against her, to taste every inch, stormed over her.

He peeled his body from hers and sat back on his heels. He captivated her with eyes hooded beneath killer lashes as he tore off his shirt and went for his belt buckle. "Tell me then," he said, the burr of his accent thicker now as desire swarmed heavy between them. "What does that naughty woman inside you crave?"

She licked her lips as he slowly withdrew the belt through the loops of his jeans. He folded the leather in half and slapped the looped end against his palm.

"Maybe," he continued with a knowing glint in his eyes that she wouldn't answer, "Maybe she'd like me to use this belt. Give her a well-deserved spanking for leaving me hanging all those years ago. Or, better yet…" He slid his body back over hers, catching her hands in his and sweeping them above her head. "I bet she'd rather like to give up all that control. Give in a little and step over to the dark side."

She laughed, then gasped in his grip as he licked along her collarbone. "Oh, *Darth*."

The low, sexy tone of his chuckle resonated deep inside her heart. But when he somehow cinched the belt around her wrists and secured the end of the soft leather through the wrought iron frame that curled in ornate swirls above the top of the lounge's cushions, her laughter died away.

She tugged slightly, but she wasn't afraid. If anything, the way he took charge drove her passion higher.

He balanced on strong, ropy arms mere inches above her. "Trust me?"

Unbelievable—so fricking unbelievable—but, yeah, she did. "Yes," she hissed. Oh, God.

"That's what I want to hear. I'm going to make this so good for you, Eden. I have a lot of fantasies stored up. Tonight's just the tip of a very large iceberg."

"Fantasies? What fantasies?" Were they the same as hers? Oh, the things he'd done to her in her dreams.

He smiled, all diabolic and delicious. "Oh no, baby. Telling you is one thing. But showing you?" Back on his heels, he worked his fingers down her blouse, unbuttoning one delicate button after the other with slow, meticulous—torturous—movements.

"Ah, now *showing* you, that's where all the fun is."

Chapter Three

The way Shane held his breath, and the calloused fingertips he strummed along her stomach and over the center clasp of her bra, had her about thirty seconds away from begging. Begging for him to replace his fingers with his mouth and to move those talented fingers elsewhere.

Eden had never begged for a single thing in her life.

God, how did he do that? How could he, in the span of mere moments, steal her sanity so easily?

With tender strokes he pushed her shirt open and drew in a ragged breath. "You're so beautiful, lass. You take my breath away."

And then he finally did what she'd been dying for him to start all night. He lowered his mouth and placed tiny, wet kisses along the top of her breasts. A sigh gushed from her lungs as teasing hands slid down her sides and stopped at the low waistband of her jeans. He gripped her hard as he moved his mouth to a lace-covered nipple. With gentle pulls, he suckled through the thin fabric of the bra. The odd sensation of lips over lace, mixed with the strong hold on her hips had her arching into him, desperate for more of his heated mouth, for more of his devilish ways.

"So eager, too," he mused. "Easy now, there's no rush. Now that we're here, I fully intend to take my sweet time."

He gripped the button of her jeans and pulled. Holding her stare, he tugged the zipper downward. Slowly. God, so damn slowly. A growl rumbled from his chest when he finally peered at the glossy material he exposed. He bent and teased the edge of the fabric with the tip of his tongue. "Satin and lace. You're killing me here."

She pulled against her restraints. "The killing is mutual, Shane. I'm dying. I need…"

He nipped over the soft swell of her belly and curled his fingers into the denim at her hips. "Tell me what you need. Don't hold back, Eden."

She closed her eyes, arched against his mouth again and latched on to the only portion of the leather belt her bound hands could reach. She wanted to touch him, needed her hands on him, craved the warmth of his skin under her fingertips.

"You. I need *you*."

Branches and leaves rustled at the edge of the tree line. She lifted her head to look in the direction of the commotion, but instead fell victim to Shane's hot mouth as he kissed his way to her hip while inching her jeans and panties lower.

"Maybe we should go inside…" she started, her breath reacting to the seduction of his lips and tongue. If she could get him to release the belt, if she could touch him…

His words puffed soft against the skin of her upper thigh. "Why? I'm nowhere near done with you yet."

Reconsidering the decision to lead him to the open balcony, she said, "We're just a bit exposed out here is all."

He worked her pants over her ass and sat back to peel them off her legs. "I live my life in a fishbowl, Eden. Trust me, we're alone out here. It's just you and me, and probably a few lazy owls hiding in the trees." He tossed her jeans aside and caressed her inner thighs, pushing her legs open wider. "Maybe I can ask good ol' Mr. Owl how many licks it'll take until I get to your candy center."

She chuckled, loving his wicked sense of humor. But more than that, she loved the grip of his large hands on her legs, the moist warmth of his breath as it blew across her sex and the slick heat of his tongue when he finally drew it through her depths.

"Oh, *yeah*. Sweet like candy, and just as addicting."

Lost in his words, she arched her back while he licked and sucked until she damn near exploded. Her fingertips burned when she flexed and fisted her hands as he drove her crazy with his gifted tongue. Each dip into her body had her panting, tightening.

Passion surrounded her, a voracious need overwhelmed her. When he licked higher and his tongue at last covered her clit, she cried out and tugged desperately on the belt binding her wrists.

Relentless, he flicked at the tiny bud over and over. Her pussy clenched, her legs shook—she couldn't stand it any longer.

"Please..."

He licked one final time before closing his lips over her clit, sucking gently in time to a beat that could only be in his head. Tension escalated inside her, her heart raced. When he slid a thick finger inside her, every cell within her burst and she blew apart. She bucked in an attempt to bring her thighs together—the sensations bombarding her were too much, or God, maybe they weren't enough—but the width of his shoulders prevented any movement.

"There she is. Let that wild child show, love. Let her loose."

His fingers were still inside her, pressing, finding that perfect spot. He nuzzled the crease of her leg, the top of her thigh. "Another one. Come on, baby, give me another one."

The pad of his thumb on her over-sensitive clit joined the foray as he kissed his way up her body. Hot lips inched over her mound, a searing tongue dipped into her navel, sharp teeth grazed the edge of her ribs. He flicked the clasp of her bra with his free hand and finally released her to his hungry mouth.

A rough tongue caressed the underside of her breast. He pressed his thumb harder. He was pushing her, driving her higher—too high. Too out of control.

"I can't..."

"You can. You will." He captured her nipple between lips designed for sin. Shock waves raced through her when he replaced his lips with his teeth and bit. "Give me what I need. Set yourself free."

He inched to the rise of her breast and licked a path of fire over the hollow of her neck before blowing her mind by taking her mouth in a starving kiss. She moaned and he swallowed every sound. His fingers danced inside her, his thumb tortured her. Her thighs ached, her breath burned from holding it inside her lungs.

Another stronger, more powerful orgasm bulldozed over her, but he never stopped. Faster, harder, he kept going. Seconds passed, or hell, maybe minutes—time held no meaning then—and she continued to come, to writhe, to...to...

"That's it. So beautiful, Eden. So amazing."

Air finally escaped her lungs and she sucked back another deep breath. The wicked tingles inside her started to dissipate, but the harsh need for him at her core had only grown. When he slid his hand from her and gripped her hip, she met his stare and shivered at the desire and longing in his eyes.

"Let me go," she whispered, her throat dry and raw. "I need to touch you. I'll die if I don't touch you."

Without a sound, he reached up to loosen the belt. Once free, she ignored the pins and needles at her wrists and instead grasped his shoulders, pushed to roll him on his back and straddled his thighs in one fluid move. She dove for the button of his jeans while his hands fisted in her hair. Niceties were no longer required, rampant need drove her actions now.

Jeans unbuttoned, she yanked his zipper down, and they both lifted up so she could push them past his hips.

"Condom?" she asked and wriggled the fabric down to his thighs. One look at his cock, long and thick as it lay over the tight muscles of his belly, had her groaning. "Oh, mercy... Better make that magnum-sized."

She lifted her eyes to his. The smile on his lips melted her heart. "Teenage habits die hard. In my wallet," he answered.

She dug in his back pocket and handed the wallet over. Not in the least hesitant, she wrapped her fingers around him and stroked. His hips shifted under her, his eyes drifted closed. While he blindly searched his wallet, she reared back to lie between his legs. She nuzzled his length with her cheek, breathed in the manly, spicy scent of him and then took a lick.

Hard and soft. The dichotomy of the two textures warred with each other, like the finest of silks covering a steel beam. She licked again, then drew him into her mouth. He thrust upward, weaved his fingers in her hair. "Eden..."

She didn't answer, didn't want to let him go long enough to utter even a single word. All she wanted was to please him, to taste his saltiness on her tongue, to feel the harsh grip of his hand at her nape.

"Ah...*fuck*. Eden. Stop. You have to stop."

She stilled as he reached for her. He grasped under her arms, pulled her over him and rolled with her until she once again lay under him.

"You drive me crazy."

"Then why did you stop me?"

"I want... God, I *need* to be inside you. That mouth of yours is heaven, but in another fifteen seconds..." He ripped the condom packet with his teeth and covered himself. "Well, let's just say I don't want my command performance to be over too quickly."

With an elbow under her knee, he lifted her leg, looked into her eyes and thrust, inch by luscious inch, until he settled himself deep inside her. She clutched his biceps, broke from his stare and bowed into him as he pressed into her again and again. When he kissed her, they moaned as one, their mouths and tongues dancing in harmony as unexpected sensations exploded between them.

They fit together perfectly, her and this rock-star bad boy. Breaths melded, sighs and groaned words of passion merged until she had no clue of up, in, down, or out.

Bringing her higher all over again, he palmed her ass with his free hand and shifted slightly as he ground against her, pumped harder. The angle—oh God, the angle was... just... right.

"There's another one in you. I feel it, I feel you. So hot, so tight. You're gripping me so fucking tight. Let it have you. Let *me* have you..."

Once more, she stared into his eyes through the silvery light and gave herself over to the feeling, gave herself over to *him*. He kissed her again, claimed her in every way. She tightened around his cock before breaking away to blow out an explosive cry. Every inch of her body vibrated from the raw power as they climaxed together.

He buried his face in her neck, kept a death grip on her thigh and ass as he incoherently muttered beautiful phrases in Gaelic, teasing her now with slow and tender strokes. When he stopped and eased his hands from their tight holds, she wrapped her arms around his neck. In turn, he worked his underneath her back and rolled them to their sides.

"That, sweet Eden, was worth every torturous second of wondering about you for the past eight years." He rose to his knees, pulled his jeans over his amazing rear and then stood to lift her into his arms as if she weighed nothing. "But we're not done yet," he said leaning close and brushing his lips against hers. He kissed her hard and carried her toward the French doors. "That," he grinned, "was merely the opening act."

Chapter Four

Hours later, they lay together in a tangle of sweaty arms and legs amongst the remnants of rumpled covers on the king-size bed. Pillows were strewn here and there, the top sheet and blanket had long ago been tossed off the end into a heap on the floor. The bottom sheet had even come loose and was now bunched in a wrinkle of elastic and fabric above her head. Eden felt empowered, sexy—sensual—remembering how she fisted and pulled on the soft cotton, ripping it off its corner as Shane tongued her into another erotic frenzy. The fierceness of that last orgasm, and her heady reaction not only to it but to him as well, only further added to the disarray of the bed.

Face to face now and slightly breathless, he held her firmly within his muscular arms and was dropping sweet and chaste kisses on her cheeks, chin, and eyelids when a quiet stomach rumble broke through the silence.

She smiled, wrapped her calf around his to draw him closer and draped her arm over his waist. "Was that you, or me?"

He skimmed his fingers over her shoulder and into the hair at her nape and gently traced the outline of her ear with his thumb. "Probably me. I'm starving."

Eden laughed and snuggled further into the warmth of his hold. "God, me too. But I suppose a few hours of great sex will do that to a person." When she met his gaze, his lips tilted into a seductive smile that all but screamed irresistible before he leaned in and kissed her lips, all the while massaging his fingers at a relaxing and languid pace into her scalp.

"That it will."

"I could run to the kitchen, get us something."

"Mmm…food," he said between kisses. "Food would be awesome right about now. Then after we eat, you can do that thing with your tongue again."

That earned him another laugh. "Again?"

He rolled to his back and tucked his hands under his head as she left his arms to get out of bed. Lord, he was one gorgeous man, lying there in all his naked glory, so furiously uninhibited. What a prime spectacle to behold.

"Yes, again. Repeatedly. Often. Over and over." Through the moonlight streaming in through the thin organza drapes, she caught the wink he tossed in her direction. "Stamina, babe. It's all about stamina. And that's something I have in spades."

"Oh boy." She couldn't help but laugh again. "I'm in trouble, aren't I?"

He brought one hand out from under his head and lazily scratched at the center of his chest. When he opened his mouth to speak, she held up her hand.

"Wait, don't answer that. I'm not sure I want to know how much trouble I can get into with you." And with that, she spun and headed to the kitchen.

She grabbed a container of leftover grilled chicken and a small bowl of red grapes from the fridge, set them on a tray along with napkins, a bottle of wine, an opener and two stemmed wineglasses. By the time she'd gotten back to the room, Shane had put the bed back into some semblance of "made" and was leaning back on a heap of pillows propped against the headboard, still deliciously naked. The top sheets were folded down to his feet and he'd flipped on the small bedside lamp.

"Stop," he said after she'd taken a few steps into the room. Mid-stride, she halted beside the foot of the bed.

"What?"

"Christ, just look at you."

She set the tray on the bed and glanced into the dresser mirror. "Yeah, just look at me," she retorted, pulling her mass of unruly hair away from her face and into a make-shift ponytail. Shane scooted to the end of the bed, stood in front of her and lowered her hands from her hair to fluff up what she had just tried to tame and flatten.

"Bed head. On you, I love it. It's sexy," he whispered next to her ear.

Amazing how simple words like those, coming on a quiet breath from his lips, could make her react so strongly. With heat. Longing. Such a strong desire she wanted to moan.

"You look wild. Untamed. It fits you."

Fit her? Really?

He spoke with such sincerity, completely laced with sexual overtones of course, but even at that she had a hard time believing him. The word "untamed" wasn't part of her vocabulary, the mere idea of it a completely foreign notion.

"I've never been untamed in my life. Until tonight, that is." She averted her gaze and studied his chest, traced under the cut of his pecs before sweeping her fingers over the light dusting of fuzz running down the center of his tight belly.

He continued to play with her hair and when she looked up at him, he blasted her with another killer smile. "Like I said, it suits you. You should let go more often."

Yeah, maybe he was right. Maybe she should.

She leaned over and reached into the bowl, plucked a couple of grapes from the vine and popped one into her mouth before she fed him the other. He chewed, still smiling, and sat on the edge of the bed, pulling her to him to straddle his lap. Wrapping her arms around his neck, she kissed him until another stomach growl interrupted the moment. "We should eat."

She felt the puff of his chuckle as he nibbled along her jaw. "I am."

Instead of pushing him away like she should've, she held him tighter and lost herself in the gentle meanderings of his mouth, now moving on to her neck and shoulder. "Not me.

The food." The swirl of his hands as he rubbed them along her back and then massaged his way down to caress her ass only distracted her more. But it all felt so good. At that point, she honestly didn't care if she ever ate again.

"But you taste better."

It was her stomach's turn to grumble, and she knew she wouldn't be able to get away with that not eating idea after all. "Hmm… Chicken first, me later. Deal?"

A teasing growl rose from his chest, but his hands and shoulders dropped in acceptance. "You can count on it," he said, then flopped back on the bed and raised his arms over his head in a big stretch. "What'd you bring?"

She kissed his belly, rose off his lap to sit next to him and scooted the tray of food between them. "Cold grilled chicken and grapes. Here, open this for me."

He leaned up on one elbow as she handed over the bottle of wine and the opener. He cut off the foil and started twisting the corkscrew into the top. "So…" A lazy lift of his lips led to an inquisitive gaze shot in her direction.

"So?" she countered, cracking open the container of chicken.

The cork popped when he pulled it free. He grabbed one of the glasses, filled it halfway and held it out for her. "Tell me more about Eden."

She accepted the wine he offered and tried her damndest to ignore the uneasy flutter his simple statement created. All of a sudden, she wasn't too keen on cluing him in on what she did.

"Like?" The prompt was stupid, only because she already knew what he wanted to know. But she was also willing to say anything in order to stall, even if it was only for a minute.

Pouring a glass for himself, he said, "You know, general stuff. Like how you know Greg and Ava. And what is it that you do for a living?"

And there it was, the one question she'd been waiting for. Funny how a few hours of being tangled in his arms changed the answer she originally wanted to give. Any other time she would've jumped on the question and spouted off her perfectly planned sales pitch. But now? Well now, doing so just didn't feel right.

By midnight—or maybe it had been even later than that, she wasn't sure since she'd lost all track of time—she'd already begun to have second, and third...oh hell, even fourth thoughts about mentioning her career or her company, let alone all the ideas she had for the band's next cover. After the unbelievable sex they'd shared and the instant connection she knew they both felt, she honestly didn't want to come across as some sort of letch who'd use such a powerful link as a way to further her career.

She'd worked damn hard for every professional accolade she ever received. Earned every contract with professionalism, an acute knowledge of her craft and the business surrounding it. She'd never—*ever*—stoop to sleeping around in order to move ahead. The last thing she wanted was for him to think she had.

She went for ambiguous with her response—answering, but not really answering. "I met Greg right after college. He was just starting in the music business, the assistant to the assistant of a major record producer, I think. He and Ava had only been dating a few months. She and I hit it off, connected. Been best friends ever since."

She tugged on a strip of chicken breast and tossed it into her mouth. He followed suit, swallowing before his next question.

"So, you met him less than eight years ago?"

"Seven," she clarified.

"Seven years. Long time. What have you been doing since then to keep busy?"

Ugh. How am I going to dance around this?

Even that she wanted to surprised her. Eden wasn't known for giving in or giving up. That she worried now about what Shane may think once she told him about her company, like all along she'd planned this big seduction scene just to sign his band, well what did that say exactly?

"Art. I, um… I'm into art," she hedged.

He plopped a couple grapes into his mouth, followed by a sip of wine. "Broad subject. Art, as in?"

Okay, she hated this. She was never any good at being coy, and deception irritated her to no end. "Graphic design," she blurted. "I design advertising pieces. Specializing in book and CD covers."

He stopped chewing for a moment, nodded noncommittally and then continued. "Covers?"

She took a long pull from her glass. Too long of one, probably, since the red wine now burned a trail down to her stomach. She hissed out a breath and coughed to clear her throat before she answered. "Yeah. That's the majority of my business."

"Who have you designed for?"

The question was casual, but she could tell he was fishing for answers. She blew out another breath and rattled off a few names of some up-and-coming bands.

"Wow. Impressive."

That he thought so made her heart leap. But, being that bragging was never really her style, she casually lay down on her side and propped herself up on an elbow, mimicking his relaxed pose. She ripped off another piece of chicken, took a bite, then fed him the rest and shrugged. "I like what I do."

"Me too," he said with a wink.

It took enormous effort to hold back the full-blown silly grin tugging at the edge of her lips. His comment made her beam inside. "Professionally," she clarified.

"I know." He lowered his eyes on a devilish smirk. "And these bands you've designed for," he said then, meeting her stare. "What was it that inspired you?"

Hmm. How to answer this one?

"Their music, mostly. And the feeling that runs through me listening to it. It might be kind of odd to say out loud, but more often than not the music and lyrics speak to me. You can tell a lot about what a songwriter is going through from the words and expressions they put into their music." And seeing as how Shane wrote all the lyrics for Blackguard, she knew he'd understand what she was talking about.

"So you listen. Interpret." He poured more wine first in her glass, then his. "Then what?"

Nobody had ever asked her these questions before, and she wasn't really sure how to answer so it all made sense. She took another sip, and did her best to explain. "Then I design what my heart tells me to."

It seemed like such a simple, childish answer, but it was true nonetheless. She couldn't really explain how she came up with her ideas. Once the connection came, so would the images. She'd draw them freehand on paper, or manipulate them on her computer, letting the design morph little by little into the finished creation. That's how she turned her creativity into a tangible, marketable product.

"I like that. I like that a lot." After another bite of chicken, he said, "My band's been on the hunt for a new artist. Did you know that?"

She wasn't going to lie. "I'd heard."

"Yeah, it's not exactly a big secret." He licked his fingers, his lips. The sexy way he sucked on each one, then drew his tongue across his lower lip made her want to groan. "We went round and round with the artist our manager hired for our first CD. Me and the guys, we wanted…well, something not so ordinary. Darker. Edgier. What our manager made us settle on fell short of those initial expectations in pretty much every way. It was so cookie-cutter. Typical, you know?"

"But the CD did well. You still have songs topping the charts."

He nodded. "Yeah, don't get me wrong, the album turned out great, even despite that. But the cover never really felt right. I made it very clear that we need someone who really understands who we are for this next one. Who I am." He pushed the tray toward the headboard and moved closer. So close, the combined aroma of their earlier sex drifted off both their bodies and permeated the small space that remained between them.

With an evil glint in his eyes, he tilted his glass and dribbled tiny drops of the red wine down her breast and let the streams run over her nipple before leaning in to lick her clean. "I'm thinking maybe that person is you."

Her heart rate quickened, from both his mouth on her breast and the statement he just made. "Really? How do you know?"

He shrugged a shoulder and dripped a bit more wine. "Gut reaction. I like that you design from your soul." He lifted his head and kissed her lips this time. "That says a lot about who you are."

He set their glasses on the tray above their heads and lay back down in front of her. With a gentle sweeping motion, he ran a hand from her waist down her thigh, which he pulled on top of his, and then back up again.

"Does it?" she whispered.

"To me? Yeah, it does." He yanked the pillow lying next to the tray down for them to share. "So what are you working on now?"

She tucked her hands under her cheek and edged closer to him. "I have a few CD covers contracted, and we're doing a book cover shoot next week."

"Yeah?" he asked. "Got anything you can show me?"

He wanted to see her work? Little tingles of professional pride battled with the sensual tingles his teasing touch had already created. "I have a few things on my laptop."

He nipped at her lips. "Go get it. Show me."

"Now?"

"Sure, why not?"

"Um. Okay."

He rolled away and collected the tray, setting it on the dresser while she went for her bags. When she arrived earlier, she'd haphazardly dropped her laptop case next to her overnight suitcase by the closet doors, more than a little miffed at Ava for keeping Shane's attendance a secret. All of that seemed like ages ago to her now.

She tugged the laptop from its case and turned to find Shane once again propped on a heap of pillows. "Come here," he said, holding his arm open for her to snuggle back in beside him. As they waited for the computer to boot up, she hoped the whirls and clicks would drown out the steady thumps of her excited heartbeats. God, she thought it might beat clean out of her chest.

Once the laptop powered up, she opened a program and displayed an album cover she'd recently completed.

"Eden, this is gorgeous." He toggled through dozens of screenshots, tracing every image with his talented fingers, pointing out intricate little details that most people would've never picked up on. At the same time, he unconsciously played with a strand of hair hanging over her shoulder.

"You have an amazing eye for color. Shadowy and dark when you need to be, vivid when the feel calls for it. I know the guys will relate to your style and they trust my judgment. I'd really love for you to do our cover." He met her gaze and she sucked in a breath. "Say yes and work with us."

Words left her, she couldn't think straight. All she could do was offer up a huge smile. A smile she put her whole heart and soul behind.

"I love how your designs are a direct result of your passion, a product of what you're feeling inside. And because of that, I know you're going to go places. You're headed straight for the top, sweet Eden." He kissed her then, slowly, but she also felt the stark desire lying just under the surface. "I want to be a part of that. I want to be part of you."

"Shane."

He closed her laptop and set it at the foot of the bed, then rolled back to crawl up her body, devouring every inch of her skin along the way.

Insatiable, he was so…amazingly insatiable.

She wound her fingers into the hair at his nape as he traveled higher, nipping over her breasts, and licking along the valley between them. She felt the fire from his hands everywhere at once. Her thighs, hips, ribs. When he reached her lips, she opened for him, loving the way he kissed her and the possessive way he held her.

Lordy, she had it bad.

"Mmm…" he murmured against her lips.

He pulled back a fraction of an inch, slaying her with the heat in his eyes. "Now, about that tongue thing…"

Chapter Five

Ordinarily the thought of what a typical Monday in Eden's studio entailed would put a serious kibosh on any remaining weekend happiness. This client would demand that, that client—having had the last two days to really study the proofs she sent over, thanks so much for being prompt—would bitch about this. Not so today. As she breezed through the front doors of her graphic arts studio, she knew it was going to be a day unlike any other.

Her assistant Macy glanced from her computer and grinned. With her coal-black hair done up in a spiky punk-do, she looked the epitome of young and reckless. "Looks like someone had a good weekend."

Eden returned the grin as she flipped through the morning mail. "I did. And for the record, I consider *good* to be a complete understatement."

Macy spun from her computer monitor. "Do tell."

Tapping an unopened envelope against her chin, Eden said, "Let's just say things are looking up—in more ways than one." She headed to her office. "Oh, by the way," she casually threw over her shoulder, "set up a new account in the books. For Blackguard."

Macy's scream followed her into the small room. "Blackguard? Oh my God! How? When?"

Eden rounded her desk and eased into the well-worn leather chair behind it as Macy bolted through the doorway in a flash of black leather and hot pink lace. "Saturday night, at Ava's birthday party."

Macy plopped into the chair opposite Eden. "I just knew the planets were aligned right this weekend! Don't keep me in suspense. Spill it, tell me everything."

How could she without sounding even giddier than Macy was already acting? "Nothing's signed, nothing's official yet. I…I can't really explain it."

"Try, please! You met them? You met the band?"

"I met the band," she answered, doing her damnedest to sound professional despite the flutters in her stomach. She reached across the desk to power up her computer.

"All of them?"

Eden laughed. "No, not all of them. Just Shane and Brett."

Macy flopped back in the chair. "I can't believe it. Finally. You finally met with Shane Tolan and Brett O'Neal. So how was it? What are they like? How'd you pitch your ideas?"

Damn, loaded questions, all of them. "Well, I really just skimmed over my ideas," she replied, being evasive while struggling to keep a blush from coloring her cheeks.

After she'd shown Shane the pieces on her laptop, they'd ended up talking further about her thoughts for the band's next cover. Their ideas, as it turned out, were actually quite similar. In between more kisses, caresses and another round of amazing sex, she believed she had a fairly good grasp of what he wanted, of what it was that made Shane Tolan tick. Both professionally as well as personally.

Especially personally, she thought, getting warm all over again remembering the way his body tightened as she took him in her mouth, the deep groans rising from inside his chest, the way he held her hair back in a clenched fist so he could watch her…

"Hello? Earth to Eden." Macy's chuckle brought her back to the here and now. "What did they say?"

Eden cleared her throat and attempted to calm her now hammering heart, feeling a bit awkward that she'd been caught so blatantly daydreaming. "I was, um, able to show

Shane a couple things on my laptop, which he really liked. Actually, he's due here in a couple hours to look over the specifics I have started for their new CD. Barring any issues the other band members may have, I'd say we're a go for this project."

Macy beamed. "This is just amazing. Is Brett coming with him?"

Well, seemed as though Eden wasn't the only woman she knew with a thing for rockers. "Sorry to disappoint, but my meeting is with Shane." A little meeting, a little lunch… Then a whole lot of one-on-one time. Eden couldn't wait. She smiled over at the crestfallen Macy. "Maybe I can see if we can set something up for later in the week, bring in the whole band."

Macy grinned before feigning interest in her matching neon-pink fingernails. "Yeah, that's a great idea. We always do our best work with the clients we know personally. Right?"

They both laughed at the unspoken meaning. Eden's fun screeched to a halt, however, the moment she opened her email program. There had to be at least twenty emails from Ava, the first one sent at six that morning, the remainder delivered at ten-minute intervals after that.

"What the…" She clicked on the first one to open it.

Eden! Where are you? Why aren't you answering your phone? Do not do or say anything until I talk to you! Call me.

Eden pulled her cell phone from her purse and checked the display. Dead. Figures. In the midst of her wild weekend, she'd forgotten to charge it. She clicked on the next email and found more of the same. What on earth had Ava so desperate to talk to her?

"Have you taken the phone off the answering service yet this morning?" she asked Macy.

"No, not yet. I started right in on the graphics for the new compilation CD when I got here. Sorry, it completely slipped my mind."

About to ask Macy to check with the answering service now, she froze when a new email from a rival at a leading art studio popped into her inbox. Panic replaced curiosity as she read it, the snarkiness of each word coming through as if they'd been spoken out loud.

Well, this is certainly one way to win a client. Beautifully played, wonderfully down and dirty, Eden. Hope it all works out for you. T.K.

Eden stared at the blue website link below the message. All the happiness she'd felt, the way her life had somehow evened out over the weekend, shattered into oblivion once she clicked on the underlined words.

A sleazy paparazzi-hungry gossip website opened in a new window. At the top—in full-on night-vision-green glory—was a picture of her and Shane. They were both naked, with her leg draped over his arm and her head tossed back on the cushion of the chaise lounge. The angle of his biceps covered her breast and the side of his hip hid the rest of her, but it was very obvious what they were doing.

Blood rushed from her head as rage rose in her throat. The noise that night, that quiet rustle in the leaves at the edge of the tree line she'd heard. It had been a fucking photographer. "God, no."

"Eden?"

Macy's voice sounded a million miles away as Eden helplessly stared at the picture. Underneath were thumbnails for a half-dozen other shots. She clicked each one in turn, reading captions of how *Hot Rocker Shane Tolan of Blackguard and graphic artist Eden Foster melted this photographer's lens with a liaison so hot it would make even the calmest night creature blush.*

Macy rushed behind her and peered at the monitor from over her shoulder. "Oh shit," she whispered.

Stunned, shocked—*mortified*—Eden forced the pointer of the mouse over the last image and clicked. Shane's eyes glowed an eerie green from looking in the direction of the camera. Her thigh suddenly cramped where his fingers dug into her flesh in the picture, her shoulder ached where his teeth had latched onto her skin. The description under the photo simply read, *"Smile for the camera, Shane."*

"Yeah," she blew out. "Oh shit is right."

* * * * *

Thank God Eden could count on Macy. She squeezed Eden's shoulder, said, "I'll go run interference," and headed back out to the main office, closing the door gently as she left.

Eden couldn't take her eyes off the monitor. The nasty e-mail message combined with the telling pictures said it all—the credibility she struggled for so many years to build just burst into a fireball in her face. Everything she'd worked so hard to accomplish, every personal sacrifice she'd ever made would be scattered to the four winds like the proverbial ashes they now were.

The first time I give up control, let loose and live a little for myself, and look what happens.

The pinpoint glow of Shane's eyes in that last picture niggled at the back of her mind. She wanted to believe he'd never willingly set her up for something shady like this, but the way he stared in the direction of the camera had unwelcome doubts circling the edges of her thoughts.

After all, there was no such thing as bad publicity, right?

As she figured would happen, the phone lines rang off the hook the second Macy took them off the answering service. All three lit up simultaneously, and Eden cradled her forehead in her hands as Macy's muffled pat responses to the callers drifted through the closed door.

"Ms. Foster has no comment at this time."

"I'm sorry, no statement will be made."

"Ms. Foster is not taking calls."

After twenty or so identical responses, Eden's head snapped up when Macy's tone changed. "Mr. Tolan? Let me put you on hold. Yes, yes…just a moment, please."

Macy knocked softly, cracked open the door and poked her head in. "Eden, it's him. Do you want me to put the call through?"

Oh hell, did she?

Through all the misgivings firing in her brain, the answer came swiftly enough. She nodded to Macy, who turned and went back to her desk.

Eden steeled herself and picked up the receiver on the first ring.

"Eden? Are you okay?" A tinge of anger edged Shane's voice. "Tell me these bastards haven't been hounding you all morning."

"I'm fine. A bit shocked, but I'm all right."

A deep breath sounded over the line. "Hell, baby. I'm sorry. So damn sorry. Brett and I were so careful when we drove out there, I was absolutely certain the car hadn't been followed. But every now and again one of these jerk-offs sneaks in under our radar. It's my fault you got caught in the middle of this. I should've been more careful, protected you from the possibility."

The honest sincerity in his tone chipped away at the doubts in her mind. She mimicked his weary breath, knowing in her heart he hadn't purposely sold her out.

"No one can blame you for wanting to live a relatively normal life, Shane. I don't hold you responsible. We both made the decision to be outside."

His voice took a sultry turn. "Current circumstances aside, it was the best decision I ever made." He paused and she heard a door closing on his end. "I want you again, Eden. I've thought of little else since you went home last night. Come to my place. We'll lay low for a while, work on the cover for the CD—while we work on each other."

God, how she'd love to. She got a heated rush just from thinking about it. But then she peered toward her computer with the email from her rival open in one window, the website with the pictures open in another.

Her flawless reputation for professionalism was on the line here. Could she risk damaging that, risk the possibility that her faithful clients might see these photos, come to their own conclusions and view her as someone she truly wasn't? Could she handle it if in the end, they thought the worst of her?

Was she willing to risk all that for Shane?

"Eden?"

Torn between the ache in her heart and the unease in her mind, it took her a moment to answer. "I don't know if I can do that," she finally whispered into the receiver. "I just don't know if I can."

Chapter Six

Eden made a beeline straight for the minibar in her kitchen once she arrived home. Shane hadn't been pleased with her answer, and had been even less thrilled when she'd told him not to come by the office for their scheduled appointment.

"Eden, this is crazy. The media is part of my life—not a welcome one, but part of it regardless. We'll ignore them. Soon enough they'll get bored with us, you'll see."

If only that were the problem. The paparazzi and media she could handle. It was her unwillingness to let her reputation be tarnished that had her pulling away now. If this were only about Shane, about the possibility of starting a relationship with him, she could easily put all the unpleasant aspects of his super-stardom out of her mind and deal with it.

But that simply wasn't the case. Not anymore.

Her character, her control, could be crushed by this. By her one night—albeit her one *amazing* night—of self-indulgence. How could she overcome the internal guilt of something like that?

She'd have to give up the CD cover, that was clear. And she wouldn't be able to see him for a while either. Not with the way gossip columnists could hammer on and on with their speculative innuendos. Their made-up stories and lies alone would be enough to contaminate her precious reputation for self-control and the professionalism she had worked for years to build. She needed to put a little distance between them right now. Give it some time, let the dust settle.

Still, the mere idea of not feeling his hands on her skin again, of not having his lips brush against hers or being able to laugh at his quick sense of humor left a gnawing hole inside her so deep and cold, she was afraid nothing would warm or fill it.

But she had no other choice. Her business, her livelihood, had to come before any personal happiness she may crave.

She uncorked a bottle of red, grabbed a wineglass and made her way to the veranda outside the kitchen door. Groaning, she curled both legs beneath her at the patio table, tired and beat to hell from the shitty turns the day had taken. With every sip she attempted to force from her mind the annoying crap bogging her down. She reveled in the quiet at first, but within moments a leery sense of vulnerability poked at the back of her imagination. Even though she lived in a private community, the events of today would make it difficult to ever trust being outdoors again.

Well, at least this time I have all my clothes on.

The thought held such creepiness it compelled her to scan the backyard. The area was small, closed in by an eight-foot-tall privacy fence, with large flowering bushes along the back edge and a decades-old lime tree in the corner. Certainly enough places for a determined photographer to hide, but the breeze was calm and nothing stirred within the leaves.

"Oh, for heaven's sake. I'm being ridiculous." Even so, she grabbed the bottle and her glass and headed back inside. As she stepped over the threshold, a booming rap at the front door shook the walls of the entryway and scared the living daylights out of her. Wine sloshed over the side of the glass when she jumped and landed in a red sodden plop on her favorite white silk blouse.

"Perfect. Just fricking *perfect.*"

A sudden uncharacteristic urge to throw the bottle across the room and bask in the weird satisfaction of shattering glass flashed through her. But she slammed down the compulsion, took control and instead calmly set the glass and bottle on the end table before storming to the front door.

She peered through the peephole and froze when Shane's dark eyes stared back from the other side. All those little tingles returned in a ferocious blaze, the familiar rush of heat between her thighs, the pounding of her heart. She couldn't stop herself from turning the knob and opening the door.

"Shane, what..."

He pushed past her and his intense presence immediately consumed every ounce of air in the small foyer. God, she could barely breathe around him. He was so...big. So imposing.

So damn perfect.

"How did you find me?" As soon as she asked the question, she knew the answer. Ava. She fluttered a hand in front of her face and shot off toward the kitchen before he had a chance to say anything. "Never mind. I know how."

Shane followed her. "She's worried about you."

She twisted the cap on a bottle of club soda and soaked a corner of the kitchen towel. "I'm fine," she said, dabbing a little too roughly at the wine stain on her blouse.

He moved quietly, so stealthy she barely heard him. Her body, however, responded to every step he took, every subtle movement he made.

"Are you?" He stilled her hand and lifted her face with the gentle nudge of his thumb. "You don't seem fine. Matter of fact, you seem anything *but* fine."

Damn it, he was doing it again. Burning her with his stare, making her lose control. She didn't need that, not now. No, now she needed to keep every ounce of her rationale, do anything she could not to lose her edge. She straightened her shoulders and stepped back. "I am, trust me."

He dropped his hands and sighed. "Eden, it'll go away. In a month, no one will even remember the pictures. Everyone's attention will have moved on to the next big story. Some has-been starlet will be sucking up the limelight again, or an old freak-show child star will fuck something else up. It's just the way it works."

"I know how it works. This entire town's a rotating door of scandal and heartbreak." She threw the towel by the sink, giving up on the stain. "But that's not it, Shane. That part I can handle. It's..."

He stepped closer. "It's what?"

She studied his chocolate-brown eyes, his serene expression. She could easily fall in love with this man, and maybe a little bit of her already had.

And didn't that just figure?

Never one to hold in her thoughts, the time had come to lay it all out on the table for him. She linked her fingers with his and led him into the living room.

"Sit," she said. He did, and pulled her down with him. When their knees touched, she shifted away. No distractions, she couldn't handle that right now. This was going to be hard enough as it was.

"Look, being in control is what I do, it's who I am," she began. "I grew up a veritable hell on wheels, drove my parents crazy on more than one occasion. Tenacious, they called me, but it goes beyond that, really. It's not in my nature to stop before I get what I want, and I've never taken 'no' for an answer. I built Imagining Eden with that to back me up, worked my ass off for years to raise it to the level it's at now."

Shane remained quiet—dubious, but quiet—so she continued.

"I found out about the pictures of us through an email from a major competitor of mine. And I'm sure she got a double dose of thrill when she sent the nasty little message she penned right along with it."

Dawning crept over Shane's face. "Eden..."

She held up her hand. "If it had been only one message, I might've been able to set it aside, not taken it to heart. This particular woman has always been a pain in my ass, so I really shouldn't have expected anything less from her. But it wasn't just the one e-mail, Shane."

She'd received several more throughout the day, some not as vindictive, others even more so.

He forked his fingers through his hair and pinned her with a stare. "So you think that if you're with me, people may think less of you." He said it as a statement, not a question.

She swallowed, thankful that she didn't have to come right out and say the words. "I've worked so hard. I just don't know if I can let that part of me go."

"For me." Another statement. When she gave a tentative nod, a quick anger burned through his eyes, flushed his face. He shot to his feet, paced in front of the fireplace. "That's a crock of shit."

She stood along with him, her defenses rising at the same time. "What is?"

He stopped, fisted his hands at his sides and drew in a deep breath. "Your reasoning. A total crock. If you think for one minute that being with me or designing a CD cover for my band will somehow tarnish what you've built—"

What? He seriously wasn't suggesting that it wouldn't, not after those pictures?

"It's not about just designing a cover, Shane. It's about the perception of *how* I got the job in the first place. But that doesn't matter. I can't—"

He interrupted her with a chuckle, a sardonic sound that ate away at her temper. "You're worried that people will think you fucked me to get a contract? Honey, this town is built on that very thing."

Okay, whoa.

"Not by me! I've never dropped my guard like that, never once given anyone reason to believe I hadn't *earned*—through hard work—*every job* I've ever done. But all that's changed now. Because of one moment of weakness on my part, everything I've accomplished could be shot straight to hell."

He tightened his fists and the anger lines between his brows deepened. "A moment of weakness? Is that was this weekend was to you? What I was to you?"

"No!" She blew out an exasperated breath and plopped back on the couch. God, she was fucking up the entire conversation. "That's not—"

"You told me what you wanted. I felt your need to let go, to let yourself loose. You asked me to show you everything you'd been missing, Eden."

And she'd meant every damn word. Their time together meant the world to her, more than that even. How could she make him believe that?

Unshed tears blurred her vision and she softened her voice. "Only with you. Those words were only for my time alone with you. My work, it's a different part of me."

He relaxed his stance a fraction and rubbed the back of his neck. An uneasy, quiet laughter rose from his throat and when he moved to sit next to her, she swore he breathed out a nasty curse. "And never the two shall meet? Is that how it is?"

"It's how it has to be."

He studied her then, his devilish eyes eating her up in a way only he could manage. Gently, he cupped her cheeks and swirled lazy circles on her skin. She nearly pulled away, everything in her told her she should, but she couldn't. She wanted this one last touch, this final sear of his hands upon her skin.

"There's only one thing we can do then," he whispered.

She expected the kiss—the raw power of it, the fire that burned between them whenever they came together. What she didn't expect, what floored her more than anything, was what he said afterward.

"Baby, I'm sorry, but you're fired."

Chapter Seven

"Excuse me?" Even though she had every intention of breaking their verbal agreement, him actually out-and-out firing her had her seeing red. She was this close to taking a step back and reconsidering her decision just for spite. Nobody had ever fired her, not even the grumpy owner of the little diner where she worked when she was sixteen. And he'd had every reason to. Eden had mopped up the vat of grease she accidentally spilled for what seemed like a week straight, but he still hadn't let her go.

"You said so yourself, it's how it has to be."

She pulled back from Shane's touch and jumped to her feet. "And to throw your words back at you—that's a crock of shit."

He sucked in a deep breath and rested his forearms on his thighs. "What is it you want then, Eden? Me and what I *know* we're both feeling for each other? Or your name in the corner of a CD cover printed so tiny no one can see it?"

Ouch.

"Don't belittle what I do."

"I would never do that." He rubbed his palms up his face and pushed his fingers through his hair. "I love everything about what you do. You're exceptionally talented. I'm just trying to understand. I know your company is important to you, but..."

Something inside her shifted, gave way as if a tightly wound coil had sprung free. And he'd noticed—of that she was sure.

Just the idea of someone firing her, the tiniest hint of insinuation that she wasn't good enough to do a job—the reason why didn't matter in her suddenly irrational mind—riled her so much she couldn't think her way out of a paper bag. But even so, his ripple of perception, the instinctual way he picked up on that, rocked her to the core. He narrowed his eyes on her, examining her with such overwhelming intensity she actually stepped back. His obsidian glare bore past every one of her barriers and delved deep into her soul—so deep, so much further inside her than anyone else had ever been. A stabbing pain pierced her heart, an ice pick of truth plunging through the steel walls of control she'd erected around it so many years ago.

His eyes widened, he sat straighter.

Oh *hell*.

"Jesus, Eden. You'd do it, wouldn't you? You'd toss away everything from the last two days—the way we connected, the absolute *rightness*—all to cling to your precious control. To prove to everyone around you that they're wrong."

The words slammed into her with the force of a well-placed slap across the face. Oh heaven above. That's *exactly* what she was doing.

But she'd always done that. Always chosen her business and her reputation over any and everything that might possibly give her even an ounce of personal happiness. Dear God, she'd chosen that over what she could potentially have with this intense, passionate man standing in front of her.

And all because of an insatiable need to control everything around her—along with what everyone thought of her.

How incredibly pathetic that he never stood a chance. Not against her work, her company—or the sick idea that she actually had the ability to have power over what others thought of her.

An aching hollow of awareness seeped through her mind. How in the hell had she lost sight of the integral part of her that so desperately craved the passion he was offering? Being in control was one thing, but when had she crossed over into irrational obsession?

No other man made her feel like he did. No one had ever come close. And she'd give all that up because of potential rumors? Because of what others may think of her personally?

"You're right." She stood there in front of him with a fist pressed to her stomach, circling the drain, closer and closer to losing everything. To losing him. "God, you're right."

He covered her hands with his, pried her fingers from the fist and drew her toward him, securing her legs between his thighs. He kissed the back of her hand and the center of her palm before grasping her hips and nuzzling her stomach.

She ran her fingers through his silky hair and choked back a threatening sob. "I don't know what to say. I never meant to hurt you."

With a little lift at the edge of his lips, he gazed up at her then. "I know. And you haven't hurt me."

A tear slid down her cheek. "I don't know what to do."

He rose from the couch, held her hands in his and kissed the tear away. "Do what's in your heart."

"It's not so simple—"

He pressed a finger to her lips and unbuttoned the top buttons of his shirt. Pulling back the edge, he revealed the tattoo over his left nipple. *Blasdag*. He looked down at it, then smiled at her. Every muscle in her body slackened.

"Do you know what this means?"

She lifted her hand, a little part inside her dying to trace the beautiful black letters, to brush her fingers over his inked skin. But she stopped a hairsbreadth away and shook her head. "No."

He slid his hand up her arm and folded her fingers within his. Heat spiraled inside her as he kissed each one in turn, then gently laid her palm over the tattoo. Over his heart.

"This tattoo is for you. It means 'sweet-mouthed woman' in Gaelic. That's what you are to me, love, what you've always been. The one woman who stole my soul with a single kiss, with the sweetest mouth."

She covered her lips with her free hand as tears flowed in hot waves. Oh God, she never knew. It all made sense now. Her secret yearning for someone just like him, his search for her.

"Don't throw us away, Eden. It's taken so long for us to find each other. We get one shot at what we have between us, I truly believe that. Let's do this right, make it all count."

A deep breath gushed from her lungs. "You can't fire me, Shane." Despite her tears, she laughed at the tinge of anger that lit his eyes. He had to think she was completely daft for saying something so heartless after he laid himself wide open for her.

Laughter through tears. Who knew it could feel so good?

She held up her hand. "You can't fire me, you see, because I'd already planned to quit. But now? I've changed my mind."

The broad smile he blessed her with and his sultry, deep laughter smoothed every jagged edge inside her.

"Thank God," he breathed out.

She threw herself in his arms and clung to him with everything she had, with everything she was. He kissed her hair, her shoulder as he held her tight, clutching her in return.

"You know, in light of what's sure to be the most creative union of my life, I feel obligated to offer you a signing bonus."

She reared back, brushed her fingers along his jaw. "Stop. That's not necessary. I have everything I need right here. *You.*"

He kissed her so mind-blowingly slow her toes curled, her breath caught, and for a second, she thought she might actually swoon.

"Funny how things work out, then. That was going to be my offer. Hold on to your socks, baby. This'll be one bonus you'll never forget."

She honestly couldn't think of anything sounding better.

Chapter Eight

Six Months Later

"So, what do you think?"

Eden grinned as Shane tossed her the shiny plastic case.

Perfect. The CD cover looked absolutely perfect. Imagining Eden's name was proudly displayed in the acknowledgments, but in the end Eden hadn't designed the cover after all. Seemed she was just too busy enjoying her new man and the new life she found with him. She'd been the inspiration for the cover though, and that's all that truly mattered to her anyway.

"I love it. Macy did such an amazing job. She's blossomed so much over the last year. I don't know what I'd do without her."

"Yeah, she really rocked this out. Maybe you should offer her some sort of bonus."

Eden laughed and waggled her finger. "I should, even though that's your area of expertise. Your offers could go down in history as some of the best ever made."

"Only according to you."

She slid him a knowing glance. "Like anyone else matters?"

He returned her heated stare and her insides danced. Every time he looked at her, every time he held her in his arms, he created the same mesmerizing reaction. He cuddled up behind her now, wrapped her in his heavenly grip, and she melted. Turned into pure mush.

And she loved every second of it.

He rested his cheek on the crown of her head and rocked her in a gentle sway as they studied the CD in Eden's hands. The image of Shane shirtless—yummy in itself—cropped at his scruffy, turned cheek and again at mid-crotch, had been her idea. Macy ran with the concept and combined his sultry body, a dark and foreboding background of a high-hung silver moon, and to her surprise, Eden herself.

She'd followed Macy's instructions at the shoot and wore a skimpy black dress, draped her body around Shane's and dug a set of hellishly long blood-red fingernails into the flesh surrounding the tattoo on his pecs. The resulting photograph was dark, edgy—very vampire-meets-seductress sexy. Just what the band wanted. And since Blackguard unanimously decided to entitle the CD *Blasdag* in her honor, the premise seemed fitting, and she loved how his tattoo also served as the title on the cover.

"Man, those fingernails... I wish you would've left them on. I think I still have scars on my back from you holding on to me after the shoot that night. Makes me hard just thinking about it."

Heat rose to her cheeks, but she didn't mind. Sure, the acrylic nails had been fun, but also completely impractical. Maybe she'd try them again for his birthday. Yeah, a little treat to spoil him. He deserved it, didn't he?

She propped the CD on the mantle, spun in his arms and wrapped hers around his neck. "You get hard if I look at you sideways."

He smiled and snuck a kiss. "So true. But it's not like I can help it. Hard seems to be my natural state around you."

She wriggled her hips, applying just the right amount of pressure against the thick ridge behind his zipper. "Case in point."

His searing lips nuzzled her neck while roaming hands kneaded her back. "Mm hmm."

"And just what do you plan on doing with all that delicious hardness?" She lowered her voice, laced it with sultry promises. That she could be herself when she was around him, just let everything in her life go and *feel*, thrilled her beyond words.

When he pulled back and his fiery gaze met hers, every inch of her skin tingled. The rich brown of his irises darkened to coal-black before her eyes—a sexy trait she'd come to recognize as a sign of absolute arousal—a luscious, erotic point of no return. Easily one of the top five of the million or so qualities she loved about him.

"What do you want me to do with it?"

"God, I could think of a list a mile long," she teased.

He chuckled and held tighter. "What a little hellcat you've turned into." Winding his hands lower, he gripped her ass and ground against her in return as another grin touched the edge of his lips. "But you're *my* hellcat, so feel free to use me as a scratching post whenever the mood strikes."

"Mm... Like now?" She ran her shorter nails over the black t-shirt covering his back. At his waist, she fisted the material and pulled the offending shirt up and off. He helped her by tossing it aside. His once-even breaths were now shallow and heavy, a not-so-subtle match to her own.

When he reached for her again, she ducked from his arms and slid in behind him. The wide expanse of his back never failed to amaze her. Many an afternoon since they'd been together she'd sat behind her desk at the studio, lost in a daydream of wrapping her legs around his thighs, clawing at the delectable skin there as he made ferocious love to her.

She ran her fingertips over the hard muscles, stroked her palms up the vee his ribs and shoulders created. His hot flesh flexed and pebbled under her touch, tiny goose bumps followed her feather-soft trail up to the widest point, then down and over his biceps.

"Eden..."

"Shh." She pressed her lips against his spine, drew her tongue to his shoulder blade and nipped along the ridge of bone she found there. As if he couldn't stand not being able to touch her, he latched onto her hips, his big hands firm and strong as he curled his fingers under the tattered hem of her cutoffs.

She brushed her hands lower along his forearms, then reversed the path. She let go at his elbows, worked her way under his arms and around his sides to clutch those perfect abs. The muscles were so hard and sculpted, so much like the treasure awaiting her just below his waistband. A decadent treasure she couldn't wait to get her mouth on.

With a flick of her wrist, she pried open the belt buckle on the supple strap of leather that held so many vivid memories. Determined to banish every bad remembrance from their first encounter on the balcony, he'd used the belt with her often, sometimes to restrain her as he had that night, other times to inflict an intense sensation of pleasure/pain. Either way, the belt no longer reminded her of anything remotely traumatic, but instead had quickly become her favorite accessory.

The fly on his jeans practically unbuttoned itself with the gentlest of tugs. Without the belt to cinch them, the loose-fitting pants dropped to a heap at his feet.

Ah, *yes*…commando. Just the way she liked him.

The tight, round globes of his ass beckoned to her, and she couldn't help it—after an easy stroke over the indent on the side, she playfully smacked the fullest part of his right cheek. Shane flinched, dropped his hands and started to turn, but she stopped him with a nudge against his shoulder.

"Stay there. Let me play a little."

"For the love of… Eden…"

She laughed, a low chortle that sounded seductive even to her own ears. "Now who's the control freak? Give it up, Tolan. It's my turn."

He held his hands up in resignation. "Whatever makes you happy, love."

"This." She followed another caress with a heated whack. "This makes me very, very happy."

His chuckle morphed into a deep growl after yet another slap. Feet already bare, he kicked his jeans from his ankles and raised his arms to lace his fingers behind his head. The masculine stance he posed in created a buzz of excitement, a fluttery little tingle that traveled down her stomach to settle in a hot pool between her thighs. His physique completely enthralled her. She'd never get enough of his body, or of him.

She edged to his side and dipped under his arm to peer up at his face. His brow was heavy over his eyes and he held his jaw firm. When she spanked him again, his eyes drifted shut and he clenched his hands tighter together, an action that made every muscle in his chest ripple.

Good God.

Breathless, she dropped her gaze lower, past tense pecs, beyond the washboard abs. Below all that, nestled in a soft patch of mocha curls, she found heaven. Thick and swollen, his cock rose up over his pelvis, already weeping. She pressed the tip of her finger over the slit and swirled the hot pre-cum around the blood-filled head. He hissed, a slow and long release of a held breath as she played with him, tortured him.

"You know you're going to pay for this, right?"

It was her turn to grin. His seductive threat only ramped up her already over-the-top desire. And she knew, beyond a shadow of a doubt, he'd stay true to his word. Anticipation flared inside her. She met his hooded stare and bit her lower lip. "Can't wait."

Coming to stand in front of him, she dropped to her knees as a low rumble eased from his chest.

"Baby…"

The muscles in his thighs bunched as she roamed her hands over the fine fuzz covering his legs. Tiny hairs tickled her palms, a stark contrast to the power and strength lying just beneath the surface.

He loved when she did this to him, had said time and again that she'd twisted the original meaning of Blasdag from a simple, loving term of endearment into something sinfully hot and wicked.

Sweet-mouthed woman.

Yeah, she supposed she had skewed the gist. But who could blame her when he was the one she could put her mouth on?

She licked the crest of his cock before taking him in her hand and stroking his length. Shudders racked his body as she held him in a firm grip and sucked the head into her mouth. He widened his stance, unlaced his fingers and moaned low and long. Within a breath, he'd dug his hands into her hair—just holding, not leading. This was one area where he let her keep complete control.

Up and down, over and over, she curled her tongue just so on the upswing, only to flatten it on the down. She paid special attention to that sensitive spot on the underside where head met shaft, and teased it relentlessly. He fisted her hair, held on to her tighter. When she lifted her gaze and made eye contact, they both groaned.

"God, Ede…"

She held his stare, loving him with her mouth, but loving him even more with her heart. Cupping him gently, she ran her fingernail oh-so-softly over the seam down his balls. At her touch they drew up tight, turning into two rock-hard orbs. He adjusted his position, his breaths more ragged now, his moans louder and longer.

"Close, baby… I'm so close."

Yes, he was. Over the last six months she'd learned every inch of his body, quickly figured out exactly what he liked and knew by heart every tell-tale sign. Cradling the weight of his balls in her hand, she slid a finger further back and massaged the sensitive area directly behind them. He bucked, plunging further into her mouth. She relaxed her jaw and took him in all the way.

A primal roar rose from his chest the instant hot semen hit the back of her throat. She eased back only to delve deeper once again. His knees shook and his hands flexed in her hair from the enormous effort she knew it took to remain standing. She released his sac, grabbed the base of his cock and slowed her movements, easing him down, waiting for his breath to return to some semblance of normal.

"Dear God." He grasped her wrists, pulled her to stand and wrapped her in arms so tight she thought she might snap in half. "I swear you're going to kill me one of these days."

"But wouldn't it be a fantastic way to go?"

A muffled chuckle blew against her shoulder. "Abso-fucking-lutely."

After a moment of holding onto her, he lifted his head and peered down at her. She nearly laughed at the adorable expression of his sex-induced stupor. He ran his fingers under the thin straps of her tank top. "Baby, you're wearing way too many clothes."

Only to him would an old pair of denim cutoffs and a scrap of a tank top be considered too many clothes, but who was she to argue? She smiled, tugged the tank up and off and just as quickly shed the shorts. Fire blazed to her core as she stood naked in front of him. He looked his fill, the gleam in his eyes making her feel so sexy. So wanted.

So his.

"Much, much better." More in control now, he grasped her hand. "Come here."

He led her to the couch and laid her back among the loose cushions. She shivered at what was to come and wondered for a second if there was a word for the male version of Blasdag, because a masculine form of the term would easily fit him just as well.

He didn't say a word as he settled beside her, he didn't really have to. He knew what she craved and never hesitated providing everything she needed. They were both oral fiends, loved giving that particular pleasure almost as much as receiving it.

With his hands under her knees, he lifted and parted her legs. One thick finger teased along her entrance before stroking closer…closer… God, yes, right there. He slipped inside her, curling his finger, pressing and withdrawing at the same time. Again. Then again…

He broke the seductive silence. "Look at me."

Her heart stuttered, her breath caught. Love and passion burned from his dark eyes when she met them. He never stopped his hand and never broke from their stare.

"Keep me with you, Ede. You're right here. I'm here, too. There's only us."

Fisting the pillows at her sides, her eyes drifted shut despite his words. Whoever said payback was a bitch never had this kind of retribution coming.

"Open them, baby. You and me. Together."

Together. Yes…always. She did as he ordered, opened her eyes and held his gaze. He slid off the couch to his knees and lowered his head—so agonizingly slow and torturous she moaned at the anticipation. The tip of his tongue peeked past his lips.

And then he touched her. Her hips bucked of their own will and a guttural groan rose from her chest. He sipped from her body, nipped biting kisses over her taut clit until she couldn't breathe, couldn't think, couldn't do anything but feel.

With his free hand, he clasped a nipple between his guitar-string-calloused fingers, rolled and tugged until the tip turned a sweet cherry red, all the while continuing to rasp over that perfect spot inside her as he tongued her into oblivion. The triple dose of sensations wreaked havoc on every nerve ending he touched. She was spiraling, spinning round and round in a foggy mix of desire and lust, heightened only by an intoxicating love.

The sharp pinch to her nipple caught her off guard. The erotic pain threw her into a realm of pure bliss as he covered her clit with his pursed lips and sucked. She shattered around him, cocooned in a blanket of desire so warm, she never wanted to break free.

His eyes slid closed as his moan echoed through her body. He came over her then, digging his arms under her back to clutch her shoulders as he thrust inside her in one swift motion. She cried out as he kissed her neck, her chin, her cheek before consuming her mouth.

He pulled back and captured her heart within his gaze. "I love you, Eden. God, so much. I've finally found everything I've searched my entire life for. You, baby. It's always been you."

Tears pricked her eyes even as a smile bloomed on her lips. "Looks like your chasing days are over."

"Hmm… I don't agree."

She lifted an eyebrow. "Oh?"

He shifted and plunged deeper, playing out the tingles still coursing through her. "I wouldn't mind chasing around a few babies. Ones that look exactly like you."

Her soul melted. "You're on, bad boy."

Shane laughed. "Baby…I'm so gonna rock your world."

Oh yeah. She could hardly wait.

Also by Kristin Daniels

℘

eBooks:

Ellora's Cavemen: Flavors of Ecstasy I *(anthology)*

Getting Naughty

Print Books:

Ellora's Cavemen: Flavors of Ecstasy I *(anthology)*

About the Author

℘

Kristin Daniels has always been a reader of romance, but it wasn't until she discovered the *erotic* romance genre that she finally figured out what had been missing from all the books she'd read before. The heat, the passion…that was it! Her love of reading (any genre, any format…really just anything) led to her taking a chance on writing something of her own, and she's been hooked ever since.

Kristin calls the suburbs of Chicago home, where she lives with a hero of her very own and their three great kids.

Kristin welcomes comments from readers. You can find her website and email address on her author bio page at www.ellorascave.com.

Tell Us What You Think

We appreciate hearing reader opinions about our books. You can email us at Comments@EllorasCave.com.

Why an electronic book?

We live in the Information Age—an exciting time in the history of human civilization, in which technology rules supreme and continues to progress in leaps and bounds every minute of every day. For a multitude of reasons, more and more avid literary fans are opting to purchase e-books instead of paper books. The question from those not yet initiated into the world of electronic reading is simply: *Why?*

1. ***Price.*** An electronic title at Ellora's Cave Publishing and Cerridwen Press runs anywhere from 40% to 75% less than the cover price of the exact same title in paperback format. Why? Basic mathematics and cost. It is less expensive to publish an e-book (no paper and printing, no warehousing and shipping) than it is to publish a paperback, so the savings are passed along to the consumer.
2. ***Space.*** Running out of room in your house for your books? That is one worry you will never have with electronic books. For a low one-time cost, you can purchase a handheld device specifically designed for e-reading. Many e-readers have large, convenient screens for viewing. Better yet, hundreds of titles can be stored within your new library—on a single microchip. There are a variety of e-readers from different manufacturers. You can also read e-books on your PC or laptop computer. (Please note that Ellora's Cave does not endorse any specific brands.

You can check our websites at www.ellorascave.com or www.cerridwenpress.com for information we make available to new consumers.)

3. ***Mobility.*** Because your new e-library consists of only a microchip within a small, easily transportable e-reader, your entire cache of books can be taken with you wherever you go.
4. ***Personal Viewing Preferences.*** Are the words you are currently reading too small? Too large? Too... ANNOYING? Paperback books cannot be modified according to personal preferences, but e-books can.
5. ***Instant Gratification.*** Is it the middle of the night and all the bookstores near you are closed? Are you tired of waiting days, sometimes weeks, for bookstores to ship the novels you bought? Ellora's Cave Publishing sells instantaneous downloads twenty-four hours a day, seven days a week, every day of the year. Our webstore is never closed. Our e-book delivery system is 100% automated, meaning your order is filled as soon as you pay for it.

Those are a few of the top reasons why electronic books are replacing paperbacks for many avid readers.

As always, Ellora's Cave and Cerridwen Press welcome your questions and comments. We invite you to email us at Comments@ellorascave.com or write to us directly at Ellora's Cave Publishing Inc., 1056 Home Avenue, Akron, OH 44310-3502.